Margaret Newlands.

Prize awarded to
Mary Alexandra
            Duncan
for work in this
class – Senior $\overline{III}$ B.
June 30, 1932 .   J. L. Hardie.

SHE STOOD FIRMLY PLANTED ON THE TOP, WITH TINY MIKE BY
HER SIDE.

see page 15.

Nancy's Nephew.

NANCY'S NEPHEW

OR, MIKE'S FIRST CAMPAIGN

BY

BEATRICE MARSHALL

LONDON
FREDERICK WARNE & CO., LTD.
AND NEW YORK

Printed in Great Britain

CONTENTS.

NANCY'S NEPHEW;

OR,

MIKE'S FIRST CAMPAIGN.

CHAPTER I.

A BIRTHDAY.

MIKE was three years old that lovely August day. Three years is a long time to have lived in the world—that's what Mike looked as if he were thinking as he slowly swung himself on the garden gate, and gazed earnestly at the great blue sea, which was just the other side of the road. The golden sunbeams were having fine games with the waves, and Mike loved to watch them. The sea was his very greatest friend, next to his mother and father, nurse, and Roland, a dear old dog, big enough for him to ride upon. Every fine morning he toddled down the garden path, and clutching the gate's iron bars with his dimpled fat hands, called out—

"Dood morning, big sea!"

When he first began to do this, Janet, his nurse, had run out after him and soon carried him back to the house, cutting off any further conversation between Master Mike and the sea, but now she generally let him stay till she had got his breakfast ready. "For," she thought, "no one passing on the road dare touch him, with faithful old Roland close at hand."

"What a funny boy ours is," said Mike's mamma, as she looked out of the dining-room window and saw his tiny figure at the gate. "One would have thought he would be playing now with his new horse and bricks, and all the rest of his birthday presents, instead of dreaming in the garden."

"He's building a bridge of fancies across the sea to the horizon," his tall, handsome father said, smiling. "Come, let us have breakfast."

"I will go and fetch my boy first; he shall breakfast with us for a birthday treat this morning."

And the next minute the sweetest, clearest voice that ever a young mother had, was heard in the garden, calling,—

"Mike, my little day-dreamer, I'll catch you!"

How quickly the small dimpled hands relaxed their grasp on the gate, and what a shout of joy came from Mike's red laughing lips, as he plunged over the grass as fast as his little fat legs would carry him. It was such fun to be chased by mother! Of course the end of it was, Mike fell down in his excitement and rolled into a flower bed, and Roland pawed him all over to see if he was hurt, much to the detriment of his starched pinafore.

"My darling, now I've got you!" and he was in his mother's arms, being smothered with kisses.

Early bathers, passing on the road, turned round to admire the young mother and the boy in her arms; for they made a charming picture, with their glowing cheeks and ruffled hair.

A little later Mike was sitting at breakfast with his papa and mamma, as grave as a judge, then he was very much impressed with the honour of eating toast and marmalade "downstairs," instead of bread-and-milk in the nursery.

Another thing that made him feel very important was, when the postman came and his father's letters were brought in, there was one on the very top of the pile directed to " Michael Edward Fitzgerald, Esq."

"Who is Michael Edward Fitzgerald, Esq., I should like to know?" his father asked.

"Me, me!" exclaimed Mike.

"*You*, sir, a mite of three, with a big name like that! Take your letter, then!"

And Mike took it. His tiny fingers had some difficulty in breaking the seal. At last he managed to get his letter out of the envelope. Of course he couldn't read it—little boys of three can't read their alphabet very often, certainly not writing. But Mike thought he must keep up the dignity of the whole affair, so he smoothed out the letter, and resting his soft cheek on his little fist, he gazed gravely and meditatively at it, and then began to whisper to him·

self, as if he understood the written words. His father and mother both laughed. Mike glanced up, and blushed till he looked like a pink rose in the garden. He was afraid he had done something silly.

"Dat's how Janet weads witing," he said apologetically.

Then father and mother laughed again, and Mike hinted reproachfully in his own peculiar language that he didn't laugh when *they* read their letters! He really seemed quite hurt, but was happy enough the next minute, sitting on his mother's knee listening to the letter. It was written in an irregular childish hand, and it was only this:—

"My dearest, sweetest little Nephew,

"Billy, Kathy and I are all coming to-morrow afternoon to wish you many happy returns of the day, and to help you to eat your birth-day cake. Won't I give you heaps of kisses! and Billy says he will build you a sand fort. Mind you don't forget we are coming.

"Ever your loving aunty,
"NANCY HAYWORTH.

"P.S.—We shall come by the 2.30 train."

"Oh, my boy," exclaimed Mrs. Fitzgerald, "you are in for some hugging this afternoon, Billy, Kathy, and Nancy all bearing down upon you at once. I wonder if you will survive it!"

"What a pity, Violet, you have such a crowd of brothers and sisters so inconveniently near at hand. We can hardly call the boy our own, for the claims of these youngsters, who are all so proud of being uncles and aunts."

Mr. Fitzgerald rose from the breakfast-table as he said

this, and somehow or other his handsome face was not as pleasant to look at as it had been a few minutes before. He was not fond of children; of course he loved Mike— Mike, with his fair curls and deep azure eyes, was a child whom any one might be proud to call his own; but after Mike all children were to him romps and bears who disturbed the equanimity of life. This being his undisguised opinion, it is not to be wondered at, that he was not a popular brother-in-law among the younger portion of his wife's family.

"I wish you had brothers and sisters of your own, Edward, and then you would be able to appreciate mine," Mrs. Fitzgerald said, rather reproachfully. "Here's Janet coming for you, my darling; so good-bye for the present," she added.

Mike would have liked to stay a little while longer with his dear, pretty mother, but he, although only three years old, had learned that it is a very wise and good thing to do as you are told, whether you are exactly inclined or not. Three years is a very short time in which to learn an important lesson like this. Some boys and girls are very long over it, so long indeed that they are boys and girls no more before they have learnt it, and afterwards it is all the harder.

Mike had his morning nap, and then spent the time till dinner in playing, or rather making himself acquainted with his new toys.

He sat on the nursery carpet, contemplating a bulky

wool-lamb, and a rigid horse on wheels. Both these
animals seemed to him very unlovable at present; he was
almost shy of them, and Janet, who happened to look up
from her work, saw him stretch out a timid little finger
and touch the polished cornery back of the wooden
charger, then draw it quickly away with a shudder.

"Doesn't my pet like his gee-gee?" she inquired.

Mike shook his head gravely, and said—

"Mike wants a real gee-gee."

"But little boys don't have real gee-gees. Mike must
wait till he's a man, and then he'll have a real one, and a
carriage too, if he likes."

Janet often told Mike he must wait till he was a "big
man like his papa" to have a great many things. After
thinking over the matter—for Mike thought over everything—he had come to the conclusion that you had only
to be a man to get all it came into your head to wish for.

One night he had rather astonished his mother by
saying, as he knelt at her knee—

"Dod, please make Mike a big man to-morrow."

She had of course explained to him that he would have
to be satisfied for a long, long time to come with being
only a little boy. So when Janet said to-day, "Mike
must wait till he's a man to have a real gee-gee," he did
not feel in the least comforted. Days and weeks, months
and years would pass, his mamma had said, and he would
still be a little boy. So he sat and looked at the bulky
baa-lamb and stiff horse gravely and sadly. He could not

love them because they were shams, and he must wait for realities till he was a man.

Ah, Mike! we become men soon enough, and some would not mind being little boys again, with baa-lambs into the bargain.

After dinner Janet dressed Mike in a lovely, little out-door garment which his clever mamma had made him; in this and a big shady hat he looked more of a picture than ever. Both Janet and Mrs. Fitzgerald were deeply grateful to that hat, for it had kept his complexion safe from the ravages of the glaring sun all the summer. They thought it a great thing to have a little boy living by the seaside without a freckle on him. "Just as fair as a lily," Janet would say with pride.

"Take the children straight to the beach from the station," Mrs. Fitzgerald called from the window, as Janet was going out at the gate with her little charge, Roland bounding and barking by her side.

The station was hardly ten minutes' walk from the house, and quite close to the beach. The train was not in when they arrived, and Mike had to stand waiting some minutes. He was all impatience and excitement, not for his little aunts and uncle, but for that extraordinary thing he had been told to call a "puff-puff"—a noisy and awe-inspiring mystery to his baby-mind.

There it came at last, in a cloud of smoke and dust, snorting and panting, as if it were in a great rage at being made to stand still. The porters opened the doors of the carriages, and lots of people flocked on to the platform, but Mike's attention was riveted on the "puff-puff."

"Don't dream, dear," said Janet, "we must look for Aunt Nancy;" and she pulled him along in and out of the people.

"There he is, the little duck," exclaimed an ecstatic voice, and the next moment Aunt Nancy was making a tremendous effort to lift Mike in her arms, while Kathy and Billy did not facilitate the operation by both seizing him round the neck. Janet had some difficulty in freeing poor little Mike from these affectionate embraces; indeed it was only by taking him up in her arms that she saved him from being smothered altogether.

"Now, we will all go to the beach. You haven't forgotten your spade, Miss Nancy, surely?"

"I lost mine last time I was here; but Billy and Kathy have got theirs. I don't want to dig this afternoon; I shall sit quietly with you and Miss May, and watch."

Miss May, who was the children's governess, smiled as Nancy said this, and if you knew what a madcap Nancy was in those days you would smile too, at the idea of her "sitting quietly." It was just the very thing she had never been known to do in her life. Even in church, where every one is supposed to sit quietly, Nancy was never still for a minute, as those who took her to church knew from bitter experience. They went to the far end of the beach, and Miss May and Janet sat down in the shade of a great red cliff, and took out their work.

Billy said, "Now for the fort!" and Nancy forgot her "sitting quietly" plan, and undertook the direction of the engineers. "Kathy, you must go and collect some large stones. Billy, you must get to work at once and dig a trench—so big," and she marked a circle on the sand with Mike's spade. "Then you must both work very hard and make the fort, and when it's done I'll be a Roman general and defend it, and Mike shall be my little son and fight like a hero. Won't you, darling?"

Billy and Kathy did as they were told, for they dare not dispute with Nancy, who, although one year their senior, was pronounced greatly their superior in every respect. Billy and Kathy were twins, and eight years old. They were not by any means ideal twins, being neither alike as two peas, nor particularly wrapped up in each other. Billy was fat, and dark as a gipsy; Kathy was carroty and slight. Billy's favourite pudding was roly-poly, which Kathy couldn't bear; and Kathy had a passion for custard, while the very sight of it made Billy's little nose go in a more heavenward direction than Nature had ever intended. Their tastes were at equal variance in more elevated matters, so they quarrelled pretty often. After all, it is only story-book twins whose looks and ideas coincide so remarkably. Twins in real life are in most cases as shockingly unlike as Billy and Kathy.

Kathy went to collect stones, and thought in her secret heart that Nancy was very cool. It was no joke to build a fort if, when the laborious task was completed, you might not have the supreme fun of standing on the top of it and defending it. Attacking Nancy would be a most hopeless business, especially with only Billy to assist. And Billy thought, as he dug away at the trench, that it was very hot work, and that Nancy was taking it extremely easy. She was just throwing stones into the sea for Roland to go after. He was sure no Roman general ever spent his time in such a frivolous occupation when his soldiers were building him a fort with all their might.

"Let Mike help," said a little voice close to him, and looking up, he saw his small nephew, who had turned up his sleeves in imitation of Billy, and was prepared to dig like a man. The Roman general at last seemed to awake to the fact that his fort would never be ready if he did not lend a helping hand himself.

"Come, my men, that's not what I call working hard. Do you know the enemy is just on the cliff over there? They will pour down upon us in a minute. Hosts of great grizzly Gauls, dressed in wolves' skins! They mustn't find us unprepared; so give me a spade, and I'll show you the way!"

The twins were not as impressed with this spirited address as they might have been; then neither Kathy nor Billy had a lively, quick imagination, like Nancy, who really saw in her mind's eye a troop of awful Gauls, with fierce, sparkling eyes and shaggy hair, tearing along the cliff, all eagerness to come down on the shore and storm her fort.

"Come, you help too," she called to some other children who were digging not far off. Readily they consented, and with their aid the fort grew and grew until it stood finished, a great erection of sand and stones, with a deep wide ditch all round it. Nancy's crimson sash made a splendid flag tied to the end of a spade, which she waved in the air, calling upon the makers of her fort to now turn enemies and attack it. She stood firmly planted on the top, with tiny Mike by her side. Over and over again the enemy rushed up the sides, and were repulsed with well-aimed spade thrusts. The sea was slowly creeping nearer and nearer, which added to Nancy's excitement.

"The sea shall surround us, and we will perish in the waves, my noble boy and I, rather than give in one little bit."

"Look at Miss Nancy," said Janet to Miss May. "She does go into a game with a will."

"Yes, indeed," the governess replied; "she is a high-spirited child, and a troublesome one too; but most lovable," she added, looking admiringly at Nancy on her elevation. She stood erect, with one arm round Mike, the other wielding the spade. The breeze lifted her short white skirts and played with her long tangled fair hair; her face, not really a pretty one, was flushed with enjoyment and illuminated with intelligence—a very interesting little face to watch, Miss May thought.

"I see I must stop this game," Janet exclaimed. "I declare the sea is all round their castle!"

She rushed to the scene of action just in time to see the trampled fort suddenly collapse, and its noble defenders forced to stand with the sea over their ankles.

Janet seized the Roman's heroic son, and looked at his wet socks with much concern.

"Come, tea will be ready by this time; so we will all go in," she said. "I am sure you are all tired and hot."

The prospect of tea made the twins think of the birthday cake. With great alacrity they shouldered their spades, and bounded over the yellow sand in the direction of some stone steps which led up to the road, where their sister's house stood.

Janet followed with Mike in her arms, who repeated, in a low, tired voice, over and over again, "Mike's hot! Mike's so hot! Mike's got nasty wet shoes!"

He meditated putting his fists in his pretty blue eyes, and indulging in what he called "a weep;" but thought better of it, like a good little boy that he was.

Miss May lingered, waiting for Nancy, who stood gazing out to sea in a reverie. She was not often thoughtful, and Miss May wondered what the little tom-boy was thinking about.

"Come, Nancy," she called; "we must go into tea. Do you want to stay and see the very last of your crumbling castle?"

No answer from Nancy, who looked as if she had not heard.

"Nancy, dear, a penny for your thoughts."

This time she turned quickly round, and with a bound was at Miss May's side.

"I was only thinking," she said eagerly, shaking her hair out of her bright grey eyes, "what an awful pity it is everyone can't be great and grand. I wish I had been a Roman hero, or even to be a boy now wouldn't be so bad; anything better than to be just nothing but a stupid *little girl.*"

There was a world of contempt in Nancy's voice as she pronounced these last two words. "Now, Miss May, fork out a penny," she added, with a merry laugh. Miss May "forked out" a little good advice instead; and by the time they reached the house Nancy ought to have been convinced that a little English maiden of the nineteenth century has opportunities of being "great," in one sense of the word, and of doing all kinds of noble things in everyday life, which the Romans and other heroes of her condensed ancient history never knew anything about.

It must not be supposed, however, that Miss May was a lecturing, prosy governess, who wearied her pupils with sermons. She was just the opposite. The children loved her as well as respected her, and were quite unconscious that the lessons she taught them out of lesson hours were lessons at all, till years afterwards, when they found them more useful than all the history and geography they had ever learnt.

Mike took the head of the table at tea in his high-chair.

2

They had crowned him with a wreath of carnations and mignonette, and he made such a sweet birthday king, that his mother could scarcely pour out tea for gazing at him. Nancy thought he looked so tempting that she exclaimed several times in her energetic manner, "Oh, Mike, you darling, I could eat you up, I could."

Billy and Kathy steadily fulfilled their promise of "eating up" the birthday cake. The awe-inspiring spectacle of their brother-in-law's tall figure pacing the garden, and sometimes pausing at the bay window to nod at Mike, did not frighten away their appetites in the least. But Billy's and Kathy's appetites were not likely to be easily frightened away. They were part of their individuality. People who knew them slightly thought of them as "those children with the huge appetites," and people who knew them better could remember such a thing as their despatching a dozen buns between them, and being equal to more afterwards, only there were no more! Indeed the twins were generally remarkable for nothing but their appetites, and after juvenile parties in the winter, feats more extraordinary even than the bun one, just related, were reported of Billy and Kathy.

"Come, Nancy, we mustn't miss our train," Miss May said, after tea was over, and Mike had been taken off to bed. "We had better start at once."

"Dear Vie, do walk to the station with us," implored Nancy, with her arms round her sister's neck.

"Oh, Nancy, how you hug! As long as Mike's in the

room my collar is spared, for then you bestow all your embraces upon him. Now, leave go directly."

"Not until you promise to come to the station," persisted Nancy.

"Do come, there's a jolly Vie," chimed in the twins.

"I am afraid I shall not have time to dress for dinner if I come, dears!" said Violet, hesitating.

"No, indeed, you will not," Mr. Fitzgerald said, stepping through the window. At the sound of his voice Nancy relaxed her hold on her sister's collar, and the other children looked shy as he formally shook their little hands, and asked them how they were, as if they were grown-up people.

"You will have time to walk to the gate if you very much wish it," he added, smiling at his wife. She smiled rather sadly in return. She could not bear to disappoint the children.

"You would have come if it hadn't been for Edward," said Nancy, going down the path. "Oh, Vie, he's not a bit nice!"

"Hush, Nancy, don't let me hear you say such a thing again. Now, good-bye."

After a few more parting caresses, Miss May got her charges fairly on the road. Mrs. Fitzgerald leaned over the gate and watched them out of sight, then ran indoors, first to give Mike in his crib some more kisses, and then to dress.

It was barely twenty minutes' journey from the bright

regions of blue sea, red cliffs, and yellow sands, to the old grey cathedral town, where our friends Nancy, Kathy, and Billy lived. Their home was a roomy red-brick house in a dull square, the dreariness of which never struck the children except when they came home from visiting their sister Vie, who seemed to them to live in a different world—a world full of roses, and sunshine, and blue sea.

"I wish we didn't live in the old town," said Nancy, with a sigh, as they toiled up the stairs to bed.

"So do I," said Billy.

"So do—— " But Kathy yawned, and was too sleepy to finish her sentence afterwards.

The little birthday king lay curled up in his crib, and dreamed he was on the sand castle again, fighting his baa-lamb and gee-gee, who had, in some extraordinary way, come to life. He tried hard to drive them back with his spade; but oh! he couldn't. Then suddenly more baa-lambs and more gee-gees came—a whole toy-shop of them —forming a most irregular army. He would have been frightened and cried out, only Nancy was there, with her strong arm round him, calling out—

"Be brave, Mike! Don't mind them. I will drive them all into the sea."

And he didn't mind a bit, but only laughed at the baa-lambs and gee-gees, as they ambled about in a stiff, clumsy way.

CHAPTER II.

"TIME flies"—at least busy, happy people think so—
and when Mike reached the age of seven, it seemed
to Mrs. Fitzgerald hardly possible that it could be seven
whole years since he was a tiny, helpless baby kicking in
her arms.

He was a sturdy boy now, in blue serge clothes, made
sailor fashion; his head, which had once been such a
caressable mass of soft, fair curls, was closely cropped,
almost like a little convict's; his face was grave, but sweet
as ever, and when a smile beamed on his red lips, he looked
extremely like his mother. His home was still the pretty
house facing the sea, with the garden full of rose-bushes,
and the smooth lawn, which was becoming too limited a
playground for Mike now, for he often went to the beach
by himself, and played long, lonely games among the rocks
under the cliff.

Roland, the old retriever, was getting too aged to be
much of a companion, although, poor old dog, he would
have been highly indignant had you told him so; he
watched his young master as much as his sleepy, failing
eyes would allow him, and no doubt dreamed he was doing

21

so when he was asleep, which, to a *very* old dog's mind, is much the same thing.

Mrs. Fitzgerald had taught her little son up till now everything he knew, which, in the opinion of some admiring friends and relations, was a great deal; others said he was backward and unlike other little boys, and advised a ladies' school.

Nobody dare say this to Mr. Fitzgerald, but when his wife told him he always exclaimed :—

"Tell them I won't have him like 'other little boys;' and as long as he is unlike them, I don't mind."

So Mike didn't go to a "petticoat" school, and went on learning lessons at home. And much he loved those lessons which the dear mother who taught him made so bright and interesting. How keenly teacher and pupil discussed the history that was read every morning from nine to ten; how they laughed over the sums, which Mike liked better than his mother did; and what a wonderful aptitude he showed for remembering latitude and longitude, and finding places on the map. His love for geography was so great that he begged to be allowed to draw maps of his favourite countries; this he did very creditably for so small a boy, and wrote on a space left at the bottom all he could remember about their towns, rivers, mountains, &c.

His father, who was a great traveller, was much pleased at this, and used to tell him stories of the strange things and people he had seen in foreign lands. Mike was such an intelligent listener that Mr. Fitzgerald said one day :—

"He's the sort of boy to appreciate a cruise in the Mediterranean; I think I'll go to the Isle of Wight sometime next week, and take a look at that yacht of Hope's."

"Oh, do! A trip round the world will do us all good!" Mrs. Fitzgerald said.

"Round the world, indeed! If you are only satisfied with a voyage of that length, you must stay at home, Violet."

When the matter was settled, and it was really decided that they should spend a few months in yachting about the coast of the Mediterranean, Mike was told of the plan. His delight was unbounded, and he talked of nothing else from morning to night.

"Mother," he said one day, about a week or two before the time fixed for starting, "I wish you hadn't told me till the very last minute, for I don't think I have patience enough to last for a whole fortnight."

"I must lend you some of mine, then," his mother answered, laughing.

"I am a very lucky boy, I think," he added meditatively. "I never heard of another boy having such nice things happen to him. Uncle Hal and Uncle Billy have never been in a yacht, and they are much older than I am. I wish they could come too."

"Then you think it will be dull with no one but your old mother for a companion?"

"Oh, mother, how can you say such a thing?" he exclaimed indignantly. "I don't want them for myself, but because it would be so jolly for *them*. Do you understand now, mother?"

"Of course, I understand that you are the most unselfish of boys," she replied, kissing him.

"And that another reason why I think myself a lucky boy is that I have a mother like you, *all* to myself."

"Not *all* to yourself, young man," said his father, looking up from his newspaper. "The bigger half of her belongs to me, you know, as I am the eldest."

Then they all began to talk of the "Violet," the name Mr. Fitzgerald had given his new yacht, little dreaming that she after whom he had called her would never step on board.

CHAPTER III.

" JANET, I should like to have a donkey-ride before I go away; so, as this is the last week, I'd better go to-day."

"Very well, Master Mike," said Janet; "but I thought you didn't like the jolting."

"It isn't very nice, but then, you know, I want to say good-bye to Jack."

Jack was a donkey-boy, about the same age as Mike—a little brown, ragged scrap of humanity, who had never had a good meal in his life, nor hardly a kind word either, till he made the acquaintance of Mike and the "young 'oman," as he called Janet. Jack was not a good hand at getting custom, so stout Mrs. Jenkins said, whose donkeys it was his business to drive up and down the sands, when anyone could be got to mount them. Mrs. Jenkins sat at the stand all day long, and cast withering glances of mingled scorn and jealousy at the proprietress of a rival establishment not far off, where there were more donkeys and several boys—big, loud boys, armed with long, thick sticks, who were always to the fore with, "Donkey to-day, ma'am!" "Donkey, sir!" when a stream of excursionists poured out of the station hard by. Poor little Jack

hadn't a chance among them.   Even if he could have out-
run them to be beforehand with a customer, he would not
have done it; for those big boys had dreadful "paying
out" theories, the very thought of which made Jack
tremble.

It was a lucky thing for him when Mike and his nurse
one day happened to pass the donkey stand, just as Mrs.
Jenkins was in the act of relieving her feelings by ad-
ministering to her *employé* a most hearty cuff.

Mike had instantly stepped up to the angry woman,
and asked, with flashing eyes, why she was so cruel.

" Well, lor' there,", Mrs. Jenkins had said, rather taken
aback, "I may have been a bit 'asty; but it's rayther too
much for a body's patience to see *them* yander," jerking
her head in the direction of the rival stand, "getting all
the custom, and all 'cause a chit of a boy won't exhirt
himself.   Would the little gent like a dankey to-day?"
she continued, in suave tones.

Mike, after a little deliberation, had said he would have
a donkey, and from that day had often spent his pocket-
money on donkey rides.   Not because of the enjoyment
of the thing, for the more he rode the more he hated the
jolting.   Neither was it because he had any particular
desire to enrich Mrs. Jenkins.   No; it was for Jack's
sake that he endured it—poor little Jack, who got so
many kicks and so few halfpence.

This afternoon Jack was hanging about the stand very
dejectedly.   Trade had been very bad all the morning,

and was likely to be so for the rest of the day. Of course
Mrs. Jenkins said it was Jack's fault, and rated Jack
accordingly.

"Lazy brat," she grumbled. "Why can't ye be more
pressin' like? I'm sartin them two young ladies that
passed just now would 'ave changed their minds if you'd
gone on at 'em a bit more."

"There's the little gent a-coming!" exclaimed Jack,
becoming suddenly alert. "Hooray!" and off he ran to
meet Mike, who had just parted from Janet. She was
going to the town to do some shopping, and told Mike to
go straight home after his ride, if she was not at the stand
when he came back.

Jack knew how to make a donkey go when there was
some one on its back whom he admired and respected.
He clenched his irregular, sharp teeth together, and made
a queer hissing noise through them, which was a very
effectual way of procuring a good trot at first; but the
stick had to be resorted to when old Buzzer's—the donkey
Mike generally rode—legs began to ache, and showed
symptoms of becoming as stiff and immovable as four
pokers. Then Buzzer got such a tickling on his tail, and
such thrusts and whacks on his haunches, that he was
finally goaded into a spasmodic gallop, which was Mike's
horror, but he didn't like to say how much he hated it,
for fear of disappointing Jack, who, when Buzzer relapsed
into a sulky walk, would come panting up with sparkling
eyes, and say, burying his little brown hand in Buzzer's

mane, "Weren't that jolly, eh? My word, how he *did* go!"

To-day, however, Jack seemed to have something on his mind, and pattered after Mike on his steed with a very thoughtful countenance. Mike was only too relieved at being spared the gallop, and refrained from remarking on Jack's silence, in case he should suddenly wake up and incite Buzzer to activity. They were nearly at the end of the sands, under the shade of the cliff, when Jack came close up to Mike, and looked so inexpressibly sad and grave, that his little patron was afraid Mrs. Jenkins had been treating him very badly, not knowing how little her blows and ratings affected him; they were simply part of his life, and the cessation of them would have seemed un-natural.

Jack gave a husky little cough; it was evident he wanted to say something, but didn't know how to begin.

"Does your head ache, Jack?" asked Mike.

"No, not mine," he answered eagerly; "but Sprat's do. Oh sir, Sprat's so awful bad!"

"Who is Sprat?"

"Please, Sprat's my pal; he blacks shoes at the station. He and me have slept togither in Brompton's cellar for near two years now, and gone shares in suppers. I tells Sprat most hevorythink, and I've told 'im many times 'bout you—how you was such a pretty little gent, and spoke up so nice to me. He's been so bad, poor Sprat, that he hain't been to black shoes for more 'an a week.

This mornin' he looked ter'ble bad, and was as 'ot as red-'ot coals. I hasked 'im if I should buy 'im an horrange or somethink cool; but he says 'No, bring me the good little gent yer tells me of. Bring 'im, Jack; I wants to hask 'im a most partikler question.' I said, 'Sprat, it's himpossible. I don't a-see the young gent p'raps once in a week, and he won't come to our cellar; the young 'oman wouldn't let 'im.' Sprat, he takes no notice, but goes on a-sayin', 'Bring 'im, Jack; if you're my pal, bring 'im.'"

Jack stopped, for he was out of breath; he had spoken rapidly and piteously with a mournful appeal in his dark eyes. It was evident that he loved Sprat, whose queer name he pronounced with something like tenderness. Mike had never heard Jack say so much before, and it was with difficulty he had followed him. It struck him as rather strange that this Sprat, of whom he had never heard till to-day, should be so eager to see him; but with quick sympathy, he answered,—

"Poor Sprat, I am so sorry for him; I will ask Janet to take me to see him to-morrow."

"Come along with me to-day," said Jack, getting bold. "It ain't far, honly 'bout five minutes' walk from here. When you gets hoff Buzzer, I'll run to the corner there, and when you've payed Mother Jinks, you just come after me. I'll leave her in the lurch for once, and let her drive the donkeys 'ome alone. Won't she give it me t'morrow, though? But I don't care; she's got Jim there to-day."

Mike forgot that Janet had instructed him to go straight

home, and gave his consent to this plan.   He was anxious
to see poor Sprat, but rather in doubts about his ability to
answer the "partikler question."

Buzzer, who during the conversation had come to a dead
standstill, was now turned round and urged into a wavering
trot.   The donkey-stand was soon reached, and as Mrs.
Jenkins helped Mike to dismount, Jack ran to the corner,
where he often stationed himself to invite passers-by to
trust their bones to Buzzer's, or one or other of Mrs. Jenkins' poor driven beasts' back for half-an-hour or an hour's
pleasant jogging.

Mike joined him, and away they hurried down a turning
the other side of the railway station, which led into a street
where a great many of the people employed in fishing lived.

It wasn't far, as Jack had said, but you seemed to have
stepped from one world into another.   The sea and yellow
sands were no longer to be seen; the air was not fresh and
salt, but close and fishy; and the sun shone on dirty people
and unlovely sights.   A flight of stone steps led down to
Brompton's cellar, a roomy, ratty place, running underneath
some shops, where any little waif and stray might quarter
himself for the night rent free, undisturbed except by rats.

Sprat's couch, composed mostly of rubbish and straw,
was close to the door, for there, there was a little light,
and he could, if he cared to look, see the pavement at the
top of the steps, and the feet and legs of people who passed
along it; but to watch legs and imagine the bodies belong-
ing to them is trying work for an invalid's eyes, and Sprat

had turned his great sleepless orbs, bright with fever, to
the darkness within, which made a background to the
ghastly, fascinating pictures of his fancy.

Mike's heart beat faster as he followed his guide down
the steps. Whose fault could it be, he thought, that Jack
and his friends lived in a place like this? It wanted all
his courage to step into it for five minutes, and they *slept*
there all night; oh, dreadful thought!

"I've brought 'im, Sprat!" cried Jack, in a triumphant
voice. "Here he be, the jolly little gent, as large as
life."

Mike had to use all his self-control not to cry out when
he saw Sprat.

Jack was skinny and miserably clad enough, but what
was he in comparison with Sprat?

Sprat, as he lay stretched out on his wretched bed,
looked nothing but eyes and hair. He was much older
than Jack, but very little bigger. It was his smallness of
stature and scarcity of flesh that had gained him the name
of Sprat. He was much thinner now than he had been a
week ago, when he was running about as active a shoe-
black as his friend Jack was a donkey-boy; for fever,
neglect, and the damp cellar air were doing their worst
for poor little Sprat.

He looked up at his visitor, and his sunken eyes flashed
out like two lanterns from his haggard face.

"Ye're a little bit of a chap," he said in a strange,
hoarse voice, which sounded very much in keeping with

his surroundings; "but I swear yer'll know it. Come a bit closer."

Mike obeyed, and hoped with all his heart he would know it. Sprat stretched out five long, wasted fingers, and clutched Mike's serge sleeve, as if he wished to hold him there, in case he might disappear before he had said what he wanted to say.

"Tell me," he croaked, with almost fierce eagerness, "his it true, or hain't it true, that He'll harken to the right down *bad* 'uns?"

Almost intuitively the boy, who before to-day had scarcely known of the existence in this bright, fair world of wretchedness and ignorance, much less seen it face to face, grasped the meaning of these rough, vague words.

"He listened to the thief on the cross. There were two thieves, one on each side of Him, both nailed on crosses like He was. One was sorry, but the other wasn't. The one that was sorry spoke to him, and Jesus listened, and said that he should go to heaven that very day."

Mike spoke promptly and unhesitatingly, and Sprat relaxed his hold on his coat sleeve.

"Ah," he said, with a deep-drawn sigh of relief, and something like a smile breaking over his thin face, "he listened to a thief, did He? Then He'll listen to me, for I'm sorry. But I'm almost wusser than a thief; and, little sir, I don't know the right way to speak to Him. I heared a gent a-prayin' in a chapel once, and he screwed up his heyes, and said a lot o' long words that I didn't know the meaning of, and went on a-saying of 'em hover and hover again. Now, I couldn't do that, not how hever much I tried."

'Of course you needn't do that. Everyone may say just what they like, as long as they mean it," explained Mike; and then, regardless of his white knickerbockers, he knelt down on the dirty floor, and prayed in a clear, young voice, which echoed through the cellar, and made the gnawing of distant rats to cease, "Dear Jesus, who died on the cross for Sprat and Jack and me, who wants us to be good boys and grow up good men, and then go to live in heaven, please hear Sprat, for he is very ill, and he has got no nice home, and no kind mother to send for a doctor. Please make him well, and let him and Jack find some friends—please do. Sprat is very sorry he has been wicked, so do forgive him. Amen."

"Thank ye. That's a real good prayer, I'll bet," said Jack. "Ain't it, Sprat?"

But Sprat did not answer. He had buried his face in his straw pillow, and was using his little remaining strength to repress some great sobs. The effort convulsed his frail frame, and he was obliged to give in and let them hear he was crying. But he was soon quite calm again, and turning his face to them, which had lost the haggard, anxious look, he said,—

"It was a real good prayer. But I shan't hever be a man. I'm a-goin' to die. That's why I wanted to know hif He'd hark to bad 'uns. I want to hask Him 'fore I dies to be a bit good to little Jack, for I don't know what he'll do, poor little chap, when I'm gone! P'raps you'll

3

be kind to 'im. I fancies He's sent you here a-puppus
So it's all right."

"Oh, Sprat, you hain't a-goin' to die!" cried Jack in
an agony. "I can't roost here alone. I be 'fraid of the
rats. Oh, dear Sprat, you'll get well—say you will!"

"No, Jack, it's all hup with me," he said, his voice too
weak now to speak above a whisper. "Now, the little gent
had better go. See 'im down the street, that no one don't
touch him. Good-bye, sir; you've done me a lot of good."

"Good-bye, Sprat," said Mike. "I'll come again to-
morrow, and I will bring Janet, and she'll make you comfortable, and give you some nice things, and then you
will soon get all right. So don't cry, Jack."

He put his little cool hand in Sprat's burning hot one,
and then, refusing Jack's escort, mounted the steps, and
ran as fast as he could all the way home.

He found his mother in a great state of anxiety, beginning to think he was lost.

Janet and Mr. Fitzgerald had gone out to look for him,
one to the beach and the other to the town, the former
half-frantic with alarm. For when she had asked Mrs.
Jenkins which direction Mike had taken after his donkey-
ride, that good woman said she couldn't say, but had strong
suspicions that good-for-nothing rascally Jack had led him
into some mischief, having seen no more of him since he
drove Buzzer into the stand with Mike on his back.

"Mike, where have you been all this time?" said his
mother, who was too glad to see him all safe to be angry,

as she had intended. "How pale and strange you look, my darling!" she added, as her boy sat down and rested his face in his hands, without demanding any of the endearments and caresses which generally passed between these two after a few hours' separation.

"I went home with Jack, mother," he said. "He and his friend Sprat live in a place not half so clean or nice as our cellar. It is a shame! Why should I have everything, and Jack and Sprat nothing? It may be wicked to say it, but I can't help thinking God is unfair."

"Mike, it was very naughty of you to go anywhere without my leave," his mother replied, almost sternly. "Janet and I thought we could trust you alone, but if you run about with donkey-boys we shall be able to do so no more."

Poor Mike! It was the first time his mother's ready sympathy had failed him. He was on the verge of crying, when his father came in and reprimanded him severely for disobeying Janet, and being the cause of so much anxiety; then he broke down altogether, and went to bed in a flood of tears.

That visit to poor dying Sprat, which had seemed such a natural thing to him, was the first milestone in Mike's young life. Up till this time he had trodden a flowery, sunshiny path, with a cloudless sky above him, breathing an atmosphere of love and beauty. All the dark, sad facts of life had been veiled from his sight and unknown to his fancy. Now the way was to be difficult and often wearisome for his young feet. For a great change was to be the result of his visit to Jack and Sprat's cellar.

CHAPTER IV.

MIKE ILL.

HOW often the days we look forward to, and expect to be the happiest of our lives, turn out the very reverse. That much talked and thought of yachting expedition was abandoned, and for very good reasons. Mike had caught scarlet fever at Brompton's cellar, and when the morning came on which he had pictured himself a thousand times rising with the lark to don a *real* sailor costume, and to help Janet to put the finishing touches to the packing, to begin bidding farewell to cook, James the page, and old Roland, and to do a hundred other things, he was tossing in his little bed, chattering deliriously. His mother never left him for a moment. She turned his pillow—oh, how often; laid her cool hand on his burning forehead, and whispered soft answers to his wild questions.

Sometimes he thought he was jogging on Buzzer's back, and it was not Jack that was pattering behind with a stick, but Sprat, with his great burning eyes and flushed, hollow cheeks, calling out, "Little gint, will he hark to the right down reg'lar bad 'uns?" And Mike called out "Don't make him gallop so hard, Sprat; it makes me feel so giddy." Then the next minute he was on the yacht, sailing swiftly over the sea, which was calm and still as blue grass. Nancy was by his side with the *Violet* flashing on her large sailor-hat in gold letters. They were looking down, down right to the bottom of the sea together.

"Look, Mike, there's a mermaid; a real, beautiful mermaid!" cried Nancy, clapping her hands and laughing. "Don't you see her shining tail?"

But Mike couldn't see the mermaid, although he strained his eyes till they watered, and the sea seemed to grow quite black, and then something came bobbing up to the dark surface. Was it the mermaid? No, it was Sprat's haggard face. There was a look of agony in his eyes, and he beat the black water with his hands, and his lips moved, but Mike couldn't hear what he was saying.

"Auntie, do you see Sprat? On, Auntie Nancy, he'll be drowned!"

But Nancy took no notice; only went on skipping about the deck and laughing.

"I see the burning mountain," she shouted. "How lovely! How glorious!"

All this, and a lot more besides, shifted through the fevered little brain. The doctor looked very grave, and Janet cried, and Mr. Fitzgerald paced his study despondently. His mother nursed him, and prayed all the while. Her prayers were answered. For in a few days the crisis was passed, and Mike began to amend steadily.

"Where are you, mother?" he asked once, waking from

a long sleep, and missing for the first time the graceful
figure that had hovered about his bed all the dreary hours
of his illness.   He became frantic when only honest Janet's
freckled full-moon countenance bent over him.   " Where
is she?" he cried, starting up.   "She mustn't go away
from me!"

"You must spare her for a little time, Master Mike
dear.   The doctor said she must take some rest.   Don't
you think your mamma's tired, after all the nights she's been
without a wink of sleep?"

Mike lay down again, rebuked.   He was patient all
that day, living on the hopes of seeing her the next.

"Is dear mamma rested now, Janet?" he asked, looking
round the dimly lighted room as if he expected to see some
corner illuminated with her presence.

"No, dear," said Janet feebly, not looking at him, but
turning her head a little further the other way.   "Let us
play at the new game Miss Nancy sent you yesterday," she
went on, stealthily wiping her eyes.

"Janet, why are you so funny?   Tell me directly why
she never comes to me now, and why papa never comes
either, and who that lady is in the white cap and apron,
who popped her head in yesterday and called you out of
the room.   Dear Janet, be good and tell me everything?"

The kindly woman could not refuse her "young gentleman" when he threw his arms round her neck, and laid
his cheek, which was sadly thin and pale now, against hers.
She told him that his mamma was very, very ill, and that

his grandmamma had sent a hired nurse to nurse her, and had come herself yesterday. Sitting up so many nights had been too great a trial for her strength. "Your papa ought never to have allowed it. I saw from the beginning what it would be, and so did the doctor," sobbed Janet.

"Thank you for telling me the truth, Janet," he said in a tragic little voice, as he lay down again and turned his face to the wall. "Now I will try and go to sleep again."

He squeezed up his eyes very tightly, and Janet was satisfied. He was not sleeping all the next two hours, but thinking.

CHAPTER V.

"BE BRAVE."

THE next day the doctor said Mike might get up.
Janet made a couch for him at the nursery window,
and there he was brought, in his blue serge knickerbockers
and blouse. The last time he had worn these articles of
apparel he had looked a brown, energetic little lad; now
he was weak and weary. His blue eyes seemed larger
than ever. He looked out of the window on the familiar
landscape. Everything was as bright and gay as usual.
The sun shone on the little white-capped waves. The
sands were covered with children digging, and gossiping
nurses, and pony carriages and carts rattled along on the
road, just as if there was no such thing in the world as a
sad little boy, with a dear, dear mother dreadfully ill.

Janet was very kind. She got Mike such a nice tea;
and old Roland, who had slumbered on the mat outside
his young master's door all the time he had been ill, was
had in as a guest. He enjoyed the feast, if nobody else
did.

After tea, Janet fetched some pencils and paper, and
they played at geography game; that is, writing down as
many places beginning with the same letter as you can
think of in five minutes. Unfortunately the letter chosen

40

was H.   Janet ingeniously prefixed the aspirate to all the
villages in the neighbourhood of her native town beginning
with a vowel; thus she wrote Ainsbury, Hainsbury, and
Utton, Hutton.   Poor Mike's head ached with pointing
out the blunder, and he said he would rather play with
his new soldiers.

So things went on for a week.   Mike got up and sat
up a little longer every day, till the doctor said he was
strong enough to go away for change of air.

"And will my mamma come, too?" inquired Mike,
looking appealingly up into Dr. Fletcher's kind face.
There was a little gleam of brightness in his blue eyes,
which had been so dull and lustreless for such a long
time.

"I am afraid not, my little man; but I hope to make
her quite well for you by the time you come back," was
the reply.   Then the brightness died from Mike's face,
and a thick mist of tears gathered in his eyes.

It was all quickly arranged.   Janet was to take Mike
to a pretty farmhouse on the moors, where there were
turkeys, armies of geese, and fantail pigeons, and all sorts
of other animals.   There was a little crystal stream, too,
that Mike was to fish in with a splendid new rod his
Uncle Billy sent him.   Mrs. Bumpkin, who kept the
farmhouse, would show him how to milk the cows, Janet
told him, and the young Bumpkins would teach him to
ride the horses and to drive the carts.   Everyone had
a hand in painting a picture of this rural paradise.   His

grandmamma did the rugged grey tors, and the purple
heather. Cook, who often brought up herself the dainty
invalid dishes she prepared for Master Mike, put in the
dairy with so lavish a hand, that Mike could not only see
the terra-cotta pans, with the golden cream on the top,
standing before him, but almost breathe the cool atmosphere of Mrs. Bumpkin's cream kingdom.

James, the page, who hailed from that part of the
country, said, "Ah, Master Mike, you get somethin'
more 'an a bite in that there stream at Cragford." Which
suggestive sentence was longer than any the laconic
"buttons" had been ever heard to pronounce during his
service in Mr. and Mrs. Fitzgerald's household.

Poor little Mike, in spite of all they told him about its
charms, did not want to go to Cragford, nor anywhere
else—not even to the queenly cities fringing that far-
away azure sea, nor to the foot of great, hissing Vesuvius,
which till six weeks ago he had dreamed of every night,
and pictured to himself all day long. He wished they
would leave him curled up unheeded on the mat outside
his mother's door till she was well, and not try and amuse
him, and make him happy and strong again. He would
be content to lie there for weeks and weeks, if at the end
of them she came out all fresh and bright, as she used to
do, with carnations in her cheeks, and sweet smiles dancing about her mouth.

They were to drive in the doctor's carriage to Cragford,
and Mike was ready, buttoned up in his little grey over-

coat, straw hat in hand, some time before the hour fixed
for departure. He was allowed to go into his mamma's
room for a few minutes to say good-bye, for it would have
broken his heart not to see her before he went away. He
was instructed not to say much, but just to kiss her quietly
and come away. The nurse, in the white muslin cap and
apron, led him to the bedside. How changed she was, his
precious mother! All her thick brown hair was gone, her
face was white and wan, and the hand she held out to her
boy was almost transparent, and the fingers were so thin
that her wedding-ring slipped off and rolled away under
the bed. Mike stood for a moment rooted to the spot.

"My darling, don't you know your poor old mother?"
she asked in a weak, broken voice.

Then he threw his arms round her and covered her with
passionate kisses. His whole frame was racked with a
great sob as he cried :—

"It's all my fault, for going with Jack. Oh, dearest
mother, I can't go away, let me stay and nurse you now
I'm well."

"Be brave, like mother's own little man," she whispered
softly.

The white cap now bestirred itself, and Mike was torn
from his mother's neck. As he stumbled to the door he
heard the faint sweet voice murmur :—

"God bless my boy, and help him to be brave."

It wasn't brave to cry, so he battled with another of
those heaving sobs, and went choking down the stairs

between his grandmamma and Janet. His father came
out of his study and bade him a cold and gloomy farewell.
Cook gave him a warm though oniony embrace; and the
housemaid, speaking for James as well as herself, hoped
he would come back "fat and strong," and find his dear
mamma quite well again. Then he and his faithful Janet
were packed into Dr. Fletcher's brougham, and drove away
up the cliff road.

As Mike put his head out of the window to take a last
look at James and cook, waving their handkerchiefs in the
garden, he saw the latter in frantic pursuit of her black
lace cap, which a stiff breeze from the sea had wafted
among the rosebushes. James succeeded in capturing the
truant head-dress, and very red and discomfited did poor
cook look, as she readjusted it, for her hair was of very
scanty growth, and she was mindful of the deficiency.

At a happier time Mike would have laughed heartily.
Now he only smiled sadly, and turned his eyes wistfully
towards the sea.

It was good-bye for ever to the happy home and the
sweet young mother.

CHAPTER VI.

IS there any boy or girl, whether at a day-school or a boarding-school, or doing lessons at home, who does not like Saturday afternoon? Perhaps there are a few exemplary and studious children who would prefer having no half-holidays, but I have never met them, and never wish to meet them, for I am sure they would prove insufferable little prigs.

Nancy loved Saturday afternoons in the spring and summer, but not in the autumn and winter, for then they were spent at Mr. Daintytop's dancing-class. Mr. Daintytop, with his fiddle and exquisite patent leather toes, was one of those disagreeable things that must be endured because they can't be cured, Nancy thought.

On this particular Saturday afternoon there was no dancing-class hanging over the young Hayworths' heads. All was life and movement in 9, Abercrombie Square, that solid mansion that looked so gloomy and forbidding outside. The meal which combined the "grown-ups" lunch with the children's dinner was just over. There were the boys sliding the bannisters, and Maude and Florence, Nancy's big sisters, playing impromptu tennis over a hall-chair; and Rosey, the sister two years above

45

her in age, pounding airs from "Pinafore" on the school-room piano with the loud pedal down. The twins were ensconced in the nursery window-sill, "far from the madding crowd," sucking toffey with the utmost stolidity; while Nancy was here, there, and everywhere, making, it must be admitted, a great deal of unnecessary noise.

The postman's knock brought every one to the front-door, where a general scrimmage ensued for the letters.

Charlie was to the fore, and they were delivered into his brown hands.

"Give the letters to me at once, Charlie," commanded Maud, asserting her authority as elder sister. "I knew I should hear from mamma by the second post."

"You are sold then!" cried Charlie, triumphantly; "there's no letter for you. There's one for Miss May three for papa, and one for Florence."

"Let me take Miss May hers," said Nancy, eagerly. And off she ran with the letter up the wide staircase to the schoolroom; while the others went in a body to the smoking-room, where their father sat with his cheroot.

"How is Vie?" they all asked in chorus.

General Hayworth took his cigar from his mouth, and read some of his wife's letter aloud.

"Our dear child continues a little better, but Dr. Fletcher still thinks her in a very serious condition. She is terribly weak. Mike has gone to Cragford for ten days or longer; afterwards he will come to us, as then there will be no reason to fear infection. Dr. Fletcher allowed him to see Violet for a few minutes before he went. Edward thought it was rash, as she was much agitated afterwards. I hope all are well at home. It is indeed sad that Miss May is thinking of leaving us, but of course under the circumstances we cannot object to part from her, &c."

"Now you fellows," said General Hayworth, when he had finished, "I won't have you skirmishing about the house the whole afternoon. George, if you like, you and I will stroll down to Barnet's, and see how the puppies are going on; which of the girls will come with us?"

"Florence and I have to pay some calls;" said Maud. "So I suppose either Rosey or Nancy may go with you."

"Let me go, father," supplicated Rosey; "Nancy saw the puppies just after they were born, and I have never seen them once. Besides, I know Nancy prefers going a walk with her dear Miss May and the twins to anything else."

"Go it, Rosey," said George, a slight, fair youth of seventeen, with very long legs; "Nancy isn't here to speak for herself, so make the best of your opportunity."

"Well, anyhow, I am the eldest," said Rosey, falling back on that infallible argument which generally gained her the day on a contested point between her and Nancy.

"Go and get ready, then, my Rosebud; and understand, if you can't find your gloves we shan't wait for you."

Then they all departed as suddenly as they had invaded him, and the General was left in his glory and smoke.

What would these military heroes do if, when their suns have set and they are compelled to give up a life of unflagging excitement and activity, they had not that consoling and soothing companion—a pipe?

With soft dense clouds of tobacco smoke between him and domestic bristles and jars, General Hayworth managed to maintain his reputation as the best-tempered and jolliest of fathers.

"What a brick the pater is," the boys would often remark. And "Father's an old darling," was the constant ecstatic praise of the girls.

CHAPTER VII.

CRICKET.

NANCY waited patiently till Miss May had finished reading her letter. What a time she was! How pleased she looked, and how sweetly she smiled now and then, and why did she blush? Yes, there was no doubt about it—Miss May was actually blushing!

"Miss May!" exclaimed Nancy, when at last she folded the letter, put it in her pocket, and turned towards Nancy, trying hard to assume her governess face again, "Miss May, you look years younger than you did before you got that letter, and quite pretty."

Poor Miss May! She blushed up again to the roots of her wavy, sandy hair, and do what she would she could not prevent a great happy smile from breaking on her lips and shining forth from her kindly eyes.

"Is it decided that you are to go away? Is that why you look so awfully happy?" asked Nancy in an injured tone.

"She will share my joy with me, the dear, warm-hearted child!" thought Miss May, "so I will tell her." She closed the door, and drawing her favourite pupil down beside her on the old schoolroom sofa, she began:

"Nancy, dear, I daresay you will hardly think it possible, but all the years I have lived here with you dear children, some one has been waiting for me and wanting me. Some one, who when I was young loved me very much, but then I had others to care for me, and a happy home, and I did not value that inestimable thing—the love of a true-hearted, noble man. Yes, Nancy, I was unkind to him in my prosperity—cruel, silly girl that I was."

Miss May looked quite stern and fierce, as if she could never forgive herself, and Nancy smiled at the idea of placid, good Miss May being *cruel*.

"Then when terrible misfortune came, when my father was ruined, and died a crushed and broken-hearted man, and I was told I must earn my own living as best I could, then I knew I loved him. He could not help me then, for he was in the same business as my father, and had lost every farthing. We parted. He went out to Canada, promising to be faithful to me. I came to your dear mamma, and she, God knows, has been very good to me, and so have you all, dear. I never heard a word from him all those years, not till two months ago, when he wrote to say he hoped soon to offer me a home if I was still ready to come to him. He had been working for me, and trusting me all that time, and I had often thought he had forgotten me, and was married perhaps to somebody else. And to-day he tells me to go in the autumn to his aunt's, and go out with her to Canada; for now he knows there is no reason why I should not be his, he feels as if he could not wait another hour for me, so of course I must not delay."

The sun shone through the windows and filled the whole room. It illuminated the maps hanging on the walls, and put gilt edges to the old lesson books, so that even they seemed to rejoice for the happiness of her who had been associated with them for so long, who had been patient with them, and had never handled them roughly, or sent them flying across the table.

They sat in silence for a few minutes, Nancy gazing earnestly at Miss May. She looked at her in a new light. She had always thought her a friendless orphan, unloved outside the family circle, where she stood on a pedestal like a revered Minerva, supposed by the children as long as they were in the schoolroom to know everything. And all the time someone had loved her with that romantic sort of love which one reads of in books, and compared with it the family love seemed to dwindle down to nothing.

"Oh, how funny it seems!" was Nancy's somewhat irrelevant remark.

"Funny that any one should care for old, cross, plain Miss May. Is that what you mean, Nancy?"

"No, no! Dear Miss May, how can you think I mean that, when you know I love you? I think you the cleverest, dearest thing in the world. Cross, indeed! You are never what I call cross. I meant that it is so strange that you should never have said a word about it before, and let us think you belonged to us and nobody else. I hope he is good enough for you, that's all. Let

4—2

me hear of his being unkind to my Miss May, won't I come out to Canada and give him a piece of my mind? I believe men are all selfish, and I will have nothing to say to them when I grow up." Nancy shook her head with a worldly-wise air, as if she were the governess and Miss May the inexperienced child. She was thinking of her brother-in-law.

"Nancy, I have just told you of one who is not selfish, and there are many more like him. But come, it's nearly three o'clock. What shall we do, go for a walk or sit in the square?"

"I should like a game of cricket in the square. How jolly to think we have only a few more Saturdays before the holidays begin, and then we can play cricket all day. I will go and ask Charlie and Hal to play."

Nancy bounded away. Miss May glanced once more at her letter, and then went to fetch her hat and work.

It was not often she gave the children their choice between a walk and an afternoon in the square, for they were apt to get rather rough and shock their neighbours.

The twins were waiting resignedly in the hall equipped for a constitutional, when Nancy came down with the good news that they might take off their gloves and help to carry out the wickets, as there was to be no walk.

"How jolly!" remarked the twins complacently. But neither of them made any sign of relieving Nancy of the cricket things, with which she was grappling.

"Now, lazybones take the bat. I can't carry everything."

"I don't think I want to play," grumbled Billy, "unless I go in first. You and Hal and Charlie stay in such an age, that Kathy and I never get an innings; and I hate fielding."

"I don't mind fielding, but I *do* like batting," said Kathy.

"We always put you in first. Of course if you get out directly, it is nobody's fault but your own. But if you are going to be disagreeable, pray don't play."

And Nancy stalked off, and would have looked very dignified if she had not dropped some of the wickets. It was impossible to pick them up without dropping something else; so she was forced to accept the now readily proffered assistance of the twins, who never liked being thought "disagreeable."

Charlie and Hal and some of their school-fellows were already in the square, amusing themselves with a desultory sort of cricket; hats and coat for wickets, and an old umbrella serving as a bat.

Nancy, with her usual energy, soon organized a proper game with sides. The twins were put in first. Charlie bowled at one end and his chum Harding at the other. Harding gallantly bowled gentle underhands to Kathy, who managed to keep her place at the wickets for an over. She was warmly congratulated by Nancy for making so unwonted a stand, and blushed with triumph. Billy quaked in his shoes. It would be a disgrace to be put out before Kathy! Charlie was not so considerate as his friend, and his first ball sent poor Billy's stumps flying.

He threw down the bat, and resigned himself to fielding, very red and discomfited.

"It was too bad of you to bowl so swiftly to such a little fellow, Charlie," said Nancy, as she took up the bat.

"If you call that swift, you don't know much about bowling," was the sharp rejoinder.

"Never mind, old boy," said Hal, kindly patting Billy on the back; "you'll come off better in your second innings. Field up, and look out for catches."

Billy obeyed, and was very sprightly for a few minutes, but had relapsed into a reverie by the time a catch did come his way, and only woke up to see the ball fall at his feet.

Everybody groaned, except Nancy, who shouted "Come on!" to Kathy. She managed to run three, as Billy got flustered, and threw up the ball in quite a wrong direction.

"Billy, you are a perfect muff!" exclaimed Charlie.

Billy had nothing to say in self-defence, and resumed his post with a dejected air.

Kathy was now given out "leg before," which she declared to be horribly unfair, and she showed so much reluctance at retiring from her wicket, that she was allowed another chance. She promptly settled the matter this time by hitting her own wickets.

Charlie and Hal laughed extravagantly, and even polite Harding could not forbear a smile.

"I shan't play any more," said Kathy, with an effort at looking offended; but when Hal said—

"You know you will, Katherine; go and field at 'mid

on,'" she broke aown utterly, grinned, and blandly did as she was told.

Miss May watched the game from a seat, and was constantly appealed to as umpire. She thought rather regretfully of the time drawing near when those familiar young voices would sound no more in her ear, and when she would not be at hand to settle the little tiffs which arose (she was obliged to confess) pretty often between the children she loved so much.

The square was not very wide, and when Hal was in, the batting was so brilliant, and the fielding so very much the reverse, that the ball frequently went dancing through the railings into the road. A little bare-legged fellow in tattered garments was standing at the said railings. When the ball came near him he picked it up and threw it over with all his strength. All his strength was not much, and Nancy was struck by his feebleness.

"Look at that poor little boy, Hal, I am sure he's starving."

"You are always taken in by beggars, Nancy," Hal answered, slogging a ball with such vehemence that it rose high into a horse-chestnut tree, rustled and whizzed through the branches, and then dropped with a thud on the object of Nancy's pity. The sunburnt sticks of legs gave way, and the queer little figure doubled up and then remained motionless.

"He's hurt dreadfully!" exclaimed Nancy, impetuously scaling the spiked railings instead of going round to the gate; a proceeding which scandalized the old maid resi-

dents of Abercrombie Square, who were always at their
windows when "that wild little Nancy Hayworth" did
something more than usually outrageous.

Nancy was down on her knees trying to rouse the little
brown boy before most of the others knew what had happened.

"He be h'only stonned, miss?" said a baker's boy who
had been watching the cricket with great interest.

Yes, he was only stunned, for he opened his eyes, felt
the great lump that the cricket ball had raised on his brow
with a little grimy hand, and said faintly—

"He's a pretty big 'un, ain't he?"

"It was quite an accident, little chap," said Hal, from
the other side of the railings.   "I'll fetch you a piece of
raw beef to put on it, if you like."

"What a duffer you are, Hal! We must take him
home.   Where do you live?" asked Charlie.

"Nowhere," was the decided answer.   "I did live at
Crabstow, but I runned haway."

"I believe he's Jack! Don't you know, Billy, he drove
the donkeys the last time we went a ride with Mike.
Oh, I am sure he's Jack; you *are* Jack, aren't you?"
Kathy cried in great excitement, making a frantic endea-
vour to squeeze her angular body through the railings, to
follow up her inquiries with a closer inspection of poor
Jack, for he it was.

He gave her a sharp glance, and raised himself on his elbow.

"Yes, I'm Jack," he said, in a thick voice.   " You rode
Snowdrop, didn't you, missey? and that young gentle-

man," jerking his thumb at Billy, "Balaam; and *the* young gentleman, why he rode Buzzer; he always rode Buzzer. He was so good to me! I never see'd him agin after Sprat died, and how I did want to! Mother Jinks got wusser and wusser, and I couldn't stand her any longer. Everything got wusser without Sprat. I don't care much now what comes to me."

He finished off with a great sob, and, faint with weariness, hunger, and pain, he sank down again on the road, and closed his eyes.

"Oh, Miss May, we must take him in or he will die! Poor, poor little fellow!" exclaimed Nancy, compassionately, with her grey eyes full of tears.

"I daresay a good meal would revive him," said Miss May. "We will take him to cook, and she will befriend him, I've no doubt. Come, little boy, can you walk across the road? If not, you shall be carried."

Jack struggled on to his legs, and supported by Miss May and Nancy, reached the area steps of No. 9. Cook was called up to give her opinion. She was fat and kind-hearted, as a cook should be, and softened at once towards the poor little waif.

"I'll find something for him, Miss Nancy. My, what a bump! Come, little chap, we'll soon put you to rights.'

She took him in her comfortable arms, and disappeared with him down the stone steps. The children wanted to follow, but Miss May reminded them that it was nearly tea-time, and that they had not brought in the wickets and bats.

CHAPTER VIII.

A PLACE FOR JACK.

NANCY longed for tea to be over that she might go and see how Jack was faring, and ask him more questions. Rosey was late, which Nancy thought very provoking, for though Miss May did not wait tea, she would not allow any one to rise from the table till Rosey had done hers. Rosey was very full of her walk. The puppies were the softest, sweetest little darlings; she had nursed them all. One had taken a great fancy to her, but that was not the one papa had chosen. In a few weeks he would be old enough to come. George wanted him to be called Curly, because his hair was that way disposed, but she thought it a silly name, and would vote for Rupert or Nelson. So Rosey prattled on, consequently making very slow progress with her tea. She was rather disappointed to find the puppies not a topic of such absorbing interest as usual. Nancy, the very one she had expected to ask so many questions about them, seemed quite preoccupied, and the others were full of Jack the donkey boy, who had walked all the way from Crabstow, and who knew "our nephew."

"Rosey, do make haste," implored Nancy at last. "You must have had enough bread and jam. Begin cake now—do."

" Billy hasn't finished yet," replied Rosey. "At least he's got some cake on his plate, and I never knew *Billy* leave anything."

"I thought Jack would like it," mumbled Billy, blushing, but glad that his enormous self-sacrifice had been noticed at last.

Every one laughed except Miss May. She looked approvingly at Billy, and said—

"Very kind of you, Billy."

Rosey now becoming curious about Jack herself, made speed to finish her cake, and the whole party swept down to the kitchen. Jack, cook told them, was in a sound slumber, and must not be disturbed.

"I wish, Miss Nancy, you would go and ask your papa what I'd better do with him. He doesn't seem to have come here for any particular reason, and we can't send him back to Crabstow to-night."

"To-night! I should think not," cried a chorus of indignant voices.

"Well, if the General don't object, he can have a shake-down in the box-room for to-night. Such a morsel of skin and bone is easy to accommodate. And now, my dears, it's nearly time to be dishing up, so off with you."

"Yes, indeed!" said Susan the kitchen-maid, who was very much put out at a visitation of children so near the dinner hour. "Miss Kathy has stuck her fingers into the whipped cream, and Master Billy has eaten up all the stoned raisins."

"I've got a scheme!" exclaimed Nancy, suddenly; and then, without disclosing it to anybody, darted away.

She went to find her father. He was not in the great, red leather arm-chair in the smoking-room. He must be gone to dress, thought Nancy. All the better! If he'll let me into his dressing-room, I shall be able to talk to him without any interruption from Maud or Flo.

"Papa, may I come in?"

"Yes, madcap; you are the very culprit I wanted to collar. I hear you've been offering board and lodging free of cost in my house to vagrants. What have you to say for yourself? No, none of that hugging till you have made an explanation."

"Oh, papa, please don't joke. I want to have a very serious conversation about Jack."

"Jack! Is that the name of your pet scamp?"

"Papa, he is not a scamp," protested Nancy warmly; "he is a tiny bit of a fellow, with such soft, nice brown eyes. I am perfectly certain he is honest, for he looks straight at you. He bore the blow from the cricket-ball so pluckily, too. I am sure, dear papa, if you would only go and look at him, even you would be moved to compassion."

"Even a hard-hearted tyrant like me—eh, Nan?" said the General mischievously, with a twinkle in his clear kindly blue eyes, positively irresistible.

Nancy was obliged to abandon her gravity, and laugh as only she could laugh.

"When are we going to have the serious conversation, I should like to know?" her father asked presently as he put his studs in his front.

Nancy resumed her business-like air.

"Well, to come to the point at once, papa, I want you to vow to be on my side, against turning poor Jack out till mother comes home."

"Because then you will have no further need of my support, I suppose?"

"No, not that exactly. You know mother said before she went away that Tom was getting too old just to clean knives and boots and do messages, and that she should try and get him a place as buttons somewhere. Well, if Tom goes we shall certainly want a boy in his place. Now Jack would do beautifully. Tom could teach him his work, and by the time mother came home, there would be a boy all ready to step into Tom's shoes."

The General reminded Nancy that when people engaged errand-boys they generally went to somebody for a character. Whom were they to refer to in this case?

This was an obstacle which Nancy had not considered. However, after a perplexed pause, she exclaimed eagerly—

"Mike! He knows Jack; he was a donkey-boy at Crabstow; and Billy and Kathy remembered him quite well. Mike will give him a character, and Janet too, I've no doubt. That horrid fat old woman who kept the donkeys treated him shamefully, and the friend he used to live with died; so he ran away—he said he didn't care

where.   Oh, papa, it would be so jolly to make him
care; to make him a little bit happy, you know!"

General Hayworth was quite beaten now. He promised
Nancy to fall in with her scheme, and sealed the compact
with a kiss.   "They say she's wild and harum-scarum,"
he mused half aloud when she was gone; "but I think
she is a great deal more thoughtful than most of them, at
least for others.   She is the only one in the least like my
Violet."

CHAPTER IX.

"DON'T YOU KNOW ME?"

ABOUT a fortnight afterwards Mrs. Hayworth brought Janet and Mike to Abercrombie Square. As the cab drew up at the gate, all the aunts and two or three uncles came out to welcome them. It was a very sorrowful meeting. There was no laughter or joyful greeting, but only a silent interchange of kisses. Every one wore black. Most of the bright young eyes were dimmed with tears. Motherless Mike was wrapped in the General's powerful arms and carried upstairs to the nursery. He hardly seemed to know where he was, and looked round him without a ghost of a smile on his little rigid pale face. He seated himself on the cushioned window-sill, his favourite seat in happier days when he came on visits with his mother. When they told him tea was ready he came to the table, and ate mechanically everything that was offered him. So he went on for several days, polite and gentle to everyone, but firmly refusing to be petted and caressed, except by Janet, whom he now and then clasped convulsively round the neck. Everything he was asked to do, he did, but never once did he smile, or change that queer stony expression. The children were awed in his presence, and spoke in hushed low voices before him. They were obliged to go back to the old routine, do lessons and take constitutionals just as they had done before God took their sweet sister from them. It was a matter of course to all of them except Nancy. She chafed more than ever under the yoke of discipline, and gave Miss May a vast amount of trouble.

"Shall I mention Jack to him to-day? Don't you think it would distract him a little, Miss May?" she would burst out in the middle of a dictation lesson. "Jack would so like to see him."

Miss May's quiet "Afterwards we will discuss that, Nancy," irritated her, and I am sorry to say she would stamp with impatience, write wildly and make innumerable blunders.

Jack, owing to Nancy, was now part of the establishment. His sharpness had enabled him to learn the duties of his office with extraordinary rapidity, and his anxiety to give satisfaction was quite touching. He had begun a new life, and with the exception of Sprat's memory, which would always be dear to him, the past was forgotten.

When he heard that his first little patron had come to the house he was more than ever anxious to improve. He had not mentioned to any one Mike's visit to poor Sprat. "He might like it kep' private," he said to himself; "our cellar was a hawful place for the likes of him to see." Jack little guessed (how could he?) in what a terrible way that visit had affected Mike.

One morning, when the children were at lessons and the boys at school, Florence took Mike into the narrow strip of garden behind the house. She asked him to hold a basket while she gathered some plums. Tall as she was, there were very few within her reach; all the fruit seemed to grow at the very top of the trees. No doubt Charlie and Hal could have accounted for this phenomenon.

"It is too bad of those boys! All the fruit we have is gone before it's ripe. But I see some beauties up there. Jack must bring the ladder. Would you go to the kitchen, dear, and ask him?" said Florence.

Mike obeyed. He had not seen cook since his arrival. He remembered her of old to be very demonstrative, and rather wished Auntie Flo had not sent him to the kitchen; but he never dreamt of making objections to doing what he was asked. To oblige others was one of those lessons he had learned so early and so well that they had become habits.

"Why, I declare it's Master Mike!" exclaimed Susan, peeping round the kitchen door to see who had knocked so timidly.

"Bless his heart, so it is! So you've come to pay us a visit at last, my dear?"

Cook's arms were floury, and taking Mike's black suit into consideration, she refrained from embracing him.

"Aunt Flo wants the ladder, if you please. She can't reach the plums," said Mike.

5

Jack was called, and came with great alacrity—boot in one hand and blacking-brush in the other.

"Put them things down and take the ladder out to Miss Florence. Why, what's come to the boy!" added cook, for Jack stood rooted to the spot with a flushed, excited face, waiting to be recognized by Mike.

A neat suit of clothes and the daily use of soap and water had changed Jack a good deal; but still after a few moments' scrutiny Mike knew him. A great wave of pain passed over his little soul at the sight of him. "If I had never seen him," he quickly reasoned, "I should not have caught the fever, and *she* would not——"

"Oh, sir: don't yer know me?" asked Jack, at last.

He was very much hurt, and the tears sprang to his eyes.

"How did you come here, Jack?" said Mike, in a hollow voice.

"Sprat died that night, and I couldn't 'bide there 'out Sprat; so after a bit I runned off. I thought I shouldn't mind dyin' too, but now I'll mind, for they is all so good to me here." He finished his incoherent explanation with a sob and a grateful glance at cook.

Sprat was dead, and Jack had loved him so dearly, perhaps as much as he had loved his darling mother. Mike melted now. He threw his arms round Jack's neck, and they cried together. Cook and Susan wiped their eyes with the corners of their aprons, and Florence came in upon the affecting scene to know what had become of Mike, and where the ladder was.

After this Mike was much brighter, and talked a good deal to every one, especially Nancy.

"I would begin lessons," he said to her one day, "only when my papa comes to see me he will be sure to take me away with him; so it's hardly worth while. Poor papa, I wish he would come soon, for I want to try and comfort him."

CHAPTER X.

NANCY had a strong notion that Mr. Fitzgerald would not take Mike with him. She had heard them saying he intended going off in his yacht as soon as he could, quite alone, and that Mike was to live with them meanwhile.

"Supposing he doesn't take you, Mike?" she suggested.

He did not answer directly. His colour came and went; then, with a little angry flash in his eyes, he said—

"If he doesn't, it will be wrong and unkind. *She* would have liked me to go. But of course he will take me, won't he, Janet?"

He turned appealingly to his faithful handmaiden, who could only answer by kissing him. She knew that her master had refused to see his little boy all these weeks, and that his great sorrow had made him bitter and unreasonable.

At last there was a letter from Mr. Fitzgerald to say he was coming, but only for a few hours, on his way to Plymouth. He came just before lunch.

Mike's plate was laid next his father's, and he looked out hungrily for a few little signs of affection, but after

the very cool " How do you do ?" and kiss with which he
greeted Mike, Mr. Fitzgerald took no more notice of him
till lunch was over, and seemed quite as oblivious of him
as of the other children.

When every one rose from the table he turned to him
and said—

" I want to speak to you alone for a little while."

They went together to the breakfast-room. Mr. Fitzgerald
walked to the window, and remained there, saying nothing.

Mike had never felt so shy in his father's presence
before. He stood with his hands clasped behind his
back, resolving to be brave. It was very hard not to cry,
but he was determined he would not, because his father
had always disliked the sight of tears.

Even this room had a thousand associations for Mr.
Fitzgerald. How often during his short engagement he
had found her here, in the morning sunshine, arranging
flowers or seated at her work ! For a moment he imagined
himself standing again with his arm round the slight
girlish figure, the fresh young face turned up to his, full
of frank, confiding love.

"Oh, my darling ! my treasure ! I never thought when
I won you that it was possible I could lose you !" he
murmured hoarsely, dropping his head on his arms, which
rested on the window-blind. Then he turned round and
saw her boy. For his sake she had killed herself ! This
reflection made him blind to the poor little suffering face,
and he spoke harshly :

"I came to-day to say good-bye to you. I am going to America. Your grandmother is kind enough to say you may stay here. I hope you will give as little trouble as possible. Try and be obedient, you know."

This was a dreadful stab.

"Oh, father! you haven't forgiven me yet, then?" he cried. "I am your own little boy. Can't you love me any more? We have got no one else but each other."

It was a hard struggle to keep back the tears now. Mr. Fitzgerald made no reply; he was moved in spite of himself by the choked, earnest voice.

"I thought children got over things directly," he said to himself.

"Oh, father! take me with you. I will be so good. I will never disturb you, or do anything you don't like!"

"It is impossible, my boy. I never thought of such a thing. They surely have not been leading you to expect anything of the sort. You must go to school, and you couldn't do so if you came with me. When I come home I shall expect to find you quite a scholar." He looked at his watch. "I have only a few minutes more. Now, come and kiss me, and then go and tell Janet I have to say a few words to her."

Stooping down, he brushed Mike's lips with his long golden moustache.

With eyes full of blinding tears, cheeks flushed, and tightly-clenched fists, Mike made for the nursery as fast as his legs would carry him. He only met with one interruption on the way in the shape of tall George, who said, "Well, little Mickie, shall I carry you up on my shoulder ?"

"No, thank you, George," he answered as well as he could without sobbing, and sped on.

"That Edward has made him cry. What a selfish, grumpy fellow he is," mused George, going into a little cupboard of a room which he called his study, and banging the door. George was working up for the army examination. He went to a "coach" in the morning, and read alone in the afternoon.

Janet came away from her interview with tears in her eyes too.

"My own dear Master Mike," she sobbed, "I'm to leave you ! There's no need of me in this house where there's so many servants, and you are to live here now. Oh, dear me ! I remember I always thought I should serve your dear sweet mamma to the end of her days. So I did, but who'd have thought they'd be such short ones. But now I know she was too good and lovely for this world ! "

"Janet, he's unkind," said Mike. "But, oh ! " he added, hearing a scramble in the passage, which was a sure sign of Billy and Kathy's approach, "I want to get somewhere quite alone this afternoon. I feel so angry, and it must be wicked to be angry with him. I could get over it, perhaps, if I were alone."

"Poor lamb, I'll go out and tell them, and you lock the

door; they don't want to come in here, except to see you."

Till Mike came the nursery had for a long time been very seldom used. Billy and Kathy had occupied it longer than the rest of the family, being the youngest. They might have done so still, had it not struck them one day that members of the schoolroom proper had greater privileges than they had; so they insisted upon being recognized as part of the schoolroom body. It was a large, pleasant room, with the old rocking-horse in it, very decrepit now, on which all the Hayworths had ridden, and the rocking-chair, in which they had all been rocked when they were "muling, puking babes." There were coloured pictures of "Little Red Riding Hood" and "The Babes in the Wood" on the walls. Just over the fireplace was a grand portrait of the General in his scarlet uniform frogged with gold. It had been hung there when he went to India for the last time. That was long ago now, and only the elder Hayworths could remember papa's beard the beautiful brown the artist had painted it. The twins still came to the nursery when they wanted to play babyish games, or suck sweets in private. Of course, when Mike was there it was a popular room for everybody. When he had come to Abercrombie Square on visits he had always taken up his abode there, for granny had looked on him as quite a baby, and did still—Mike, who was so manly and thoughtful for his years!

At Janet's bidding the twins beat a hasty retreat.

They met Nancy, who had just been released from a music lesson, a thing she hated nearly as cordially as the dancing class, flying up the stairs to Mike.

"You mustn't go, Nancy. Our nephew wants to be left alone ; he's not very well," said Kathy.

"Not very well! He was all right at dinner!" exclaimed Nancy, incredulously.

"If you don't believe me, you'd better ask Janet," replied Kathy in her affronted tone. Then, seeing Billy was about to accomplish his descent by sliding down the balusters, Kathy jumped the whole flight of stairs, so as not to be behindhand.

Nancy found Janet keeping guard at the nursery-door.

"Is it true he is ill?" inquired Nancy.

"He's a little upset, dear. His pa going away, and all that, has put him about," explained Janet vaguely. "He's been so accustomed to being alone when anything's on his mind, that I thought it would be as well to let him stay for a bit. Oh, Miss Nancy, it's sad for anyone to lose a mother, but for him it's worse than for most. What they were to each other! Never a word between them, and yet she didn't spoil him one bit. Well, that she didn't, for if she had, what would become of him now I don't know! He won't even have me soon. To think that I, who have known him all his life, must leave him just now, when he'll be wanting me so much!"

"Did Mr. Fitzgerald say you were to go? Oh, Janet, he's a brute. I never liked him one bit, and now I almost

hate him. He may well be wretched and inconsolable,
for it was through his selfishness she got ill, I believe.
He said he hated sick-nurses, or she would have had one
for Mike when he had scarlet fever. I know she would,
instead of wearing herself out over him ! "

Nancy had rather a bad habit of raising her voice when
she was excited. Janet was afraid Mike might hear her,
in spite of there being a kind of lobby between the nursery-
door and the passage they were standing in.

"Hush, Miss Nancy, don't let him hear you speaking
like that. I fancy that's what he's feeling about his pa
himself, and he wants to get over it, as he says; he
always had such a conscience."

"Oh, if I could but help him ! I love him so much,
you know, Janet. I always did, as much as papa, and
more than anyone else in the world. And yet I am quite
powerless to comfort him in the very least. When I am
with him, I know he'd just as soon I wasn't there, and
he used to like me a little."

"He always was very fond of you, Miss Nancy dear,
and is still ; I think you may be a good deal to him, for
you are more like his precious mamma than any of the other
young ladies. Hester said that when she was waiting at
lunch she noticed Mr. Fitzgerald, when he looked at you,
give a start : she was sure the likeness struck him."

Nancy flushed with pleasure. "But she was so lovely,
and I am not a bit ; the boys are always telling me I am
as ugly as sin."

"Ah, they don't mean it. But try and be like her in other things besides looks, Miss Nancy."

"If I were quarter as good as she was, I should be an angel. It would be useless to try, Janet. I was born wicked, and shall be wicked to the end."

Nancy sighed heavily; then hearing Miss May calling her, she said—

"I ought to have been in the school-room long ago. I shall be safe to get a bad mark."

She tossed back her long tail of thick hair with which she had been playing as she talked, and bounded away.

Janet need not have feared that Mike would overhear them. He was lying on the floor in a passionate agony. There was a rushing, singing, sound in his ears, which deafened him. His blood boiled, hot tears rained down his cheeks, and he tore the carpet with his fingers.

"My own father doesn't love me," he moaned. "Oh, mother, mother, what shall I do? I can't forgive him. He's wicked and unkind; and I don't want to forgive him: why should I? He ought to have taken me with him. *He* is wrong, not I. How can I stay here always? Oh, it's a shame, a shame!"

CHAPTER XI.

WHEN his passion cooled a little he rose and sat brooding in the window-seat. He thought of the life that lay before him now. Only that dull square to look at instead of the great ocean, the long dreary walks through the streets before you got to anything like a green field. All these aunts and uncles, who *would* treat him like a baby, for ever buzzing round him. Nancy was better. Yes, he wouldn't mind going away somewhere quite alone with Nancy. She answered his questions without repeating what he asked to everybody, and saying:

"Isn't he wonderful? Fancy his wanting to know *that!*"

His mother had loved Nancy, but she had loved them all. He must be wrong not to love them all alike, for they were all very kind to him. He was pondering thus when Janet tapped at the door and said:

"My dear, let me come in now."

He unbolted the door, and she scanned his face anxiously.

"Ah, you won't be fit to go down to dessert. Your grandmamma has told me she would like you to go down

76

every night, and thought you might begin this evening; but, poor dear, you'll be only fit for your bed."

"Take me in your lap, Jan. dear, and nurse me, as you used to when I was a very little boy."

Janet was only too glad. He pillowed his hot aching head on her ample breast, and began to cry again, but they were not angry tears now.

"You will soon be somebody else's Janet. You won't forget me, though, even if you do get some very nice little girls and boys to look after."

"*Forget* you! You, whom I nursed in long clothes!" cried Janet. "Oh, Master Mike, my darling, how can you think of such a thing? I shall never have you out of my thoughts. As to another place, I won't take one, not if I was offered it in the family of the finest duke in the land."

"Where will you go, then, Jan. dear—home to your mother?"

"Yes, my dear, for the present." And Janet blushed.

That night when Mike was in bed Janet sat alone in the large deserted nursery, writing a letter. She laboured with a scratchy, fine pen over the slippery surface of a sheet of pale green paper, scalloped at the edges. How the fine, muscular young railway porter, who had loved Janet for many years, and insisted on being faithful to her, rejoiced over that pea-green scrawl!

"The family is broken up, John. My sweet mistress is dead, the master gone off in his yacht to foreign parts, and my young gentleman—bless him!—is too old for a nurse. If you are of the same mind as you were, John, then I am free."

Of the same mind John was, and the faithful servant became a faithful wife.

CHAPTER XII.

"WILL you allow the girls to come and see the latest addition to the family, Miss May?" inquired the General, poking his head in at the schoolroom door. It was the plain work afternoon, and all were rejoiced at the interruption. None of them were devoted to the "ladies' plough," as Mr. Ruskin calls the needle, and Nancy least of all. At Miss May's suggestion she had undertaken to make Jack a shirt; almost every stitch had been accompanied with a groan or a sigh, and Jack might well be flattered at Miss Nancy imposing on herself a task so contrary to her tastes for his sake.

"What does papa mean?" asked Kathy, not jumping to her feet as the others did, for fear it might be a "take in."

"It's the puppy, of course!" cried Nancy. "Dear Miss May, it's quarter to four; do let us go and look at him."

"Do, do," implored Rosey.

Miss May consented, but begged the work might be folded up and put away first. There were some pettish shrugs from Rosey at this delay. She was longing to be downstairs to pat the puppy before Nancy, and to be honoured by his recognitions, for she flattered herself he would remember her.

79

"How we shall manage these young colts without you, Miss May, I can't conceive," the General remarked, as the work-baskets were hastily packed and impetuously hurled into a cupboard, where they would rest in peace till next working day.

Mr. Barnet, an amateur dog-fancier, stood in the hall, holding a very youthful, loose-skinned St. Bernard by a string. George was there with his arm thrown round Mike, discussing canine "points" in a highly professional manner, when Rosey, Nancy, and Kathy swooped down, exclaiming in chorus—

"What a beauty! What a darling! Oh, let him go, Mr. Barnet, please!"

"Not in the 'ouse, young ladies; for he's not much more than a baby yet, and rather obstreporous."

"Let us take him to the garden then, and introduce him to his kennel."

Accordingly the new arrival was escorted by the whole party to the garden. On being let loose he explored his new domain, with many sniffs of disgust at its narrow limits, leaping frantically against the high red brick walls, as if he would like to knock them down and see what was on the other side.

"He's a fine beast, sir," said Mr. Barnet, watching him complacently. "Such long limbs, and a prime coat too! Come here, sir, and let's show your grinders."

The sharp, white teeth, that gleamed between the black gums, called forth loud expressions of admiration,

and Mr. Barnet, thinking that by this time he had suffi-
ciently impressed upon every one the superiority of his
charge, took his leave, promising to call in soon, and see
how he was getting on.

"George, look how well he remembers me!" cried
Rosey, when the puppy, after returning thanks for
pats by giving boisterous, foamy hugs all round, came
back to Rosey, shook her frock, gnawed and licked her
hands, and finally demanded a kiss on her lips.

"He does that to every one. But I wouldn't encourage
him too much, or he will tear your dress to ribbons," said
George.

It seemed likely that this would be the case, for
there was something about Rosey which excited the
exuberant puppy to the last degree. It was amusing to
see Rosey's delight gradually giving place to alarm. Her
repeated cries of "Down, sir!" "Naughty dog!" had
not the slightest effect on him, and he only increased the
vehemence of his attentions. Having wrenched her frock
out of his moist jaws, Rosey made a fatal move and *ran*.
Of course, the puppy pursued her, and his spirits waxed
wilder and wilder. He pawed her, tore her stockings,
jumped on her, and at last contented himself with hanging
on to a piece of flounce. In this fashion they went
round the garden several times, Rosey not daring to stop.
The General had gone into the house again, so her gasps
of "Call him off" fell on unsympathetic ears. Every one
enjoyed the scene. George shouted with laughter, and

6

even Mike went into fits. It was the first time his old hearty laugh had been heard all these weeks; Nancy, who was always on the look-out for a smile on the sad little face, was charmed.

Violent tapping at the back drawing-room window made them all look up. Maud put her head out, and said that Rosey's frock must be ruined, and how could George allow it?

This put an end to Rosey's misery. The high-spirited animal was caught and put into his kennel. Rosey, hot, dishevelled, and on the brink of tears, repented thoroughly her eagerness to claim the distinction of being recognized by the puppy! Her black satin frock now looked twice the age of Nancy's, which was a great grief to her, as Rosey prided herself on keeping her clothes in better condition than the "tomboy" did hers.

When Hal and Charlie came in from school there was a second expedition to the kennel. Rosey, it was observed, kept very much in the background, and her shrill little voice was not heard proclaiming that the puppy "would be fonder of her than anyone, because she had nursed him at Barnet's."

All through tea Rosey was chaffed unmercifully, and at last she indignantly appealed to Miss May to change the subject. Nancy tried to keep up the joke, because she hoped to see Mike laugh again as he had done in the garden, but his merriment was over, and he looked even graver and more thoughtful than ever.

Since Janet went away, Mike, at his own request, had been given the little room over George's study. He preferred having a room to himself to sharing one with Billy and Hal. Nancy on her way to bed used to look in, "to see if he was asleep." Of course he was always awake, if he hadn't been, Nancy would have been dreadfully disappointed. To-night there was a great sob before the "Come in, Aunt Nancy."

"Why, Mike, darling, are you crying?" she asked, throwing herself on her knees by the bedside and feeling for his hand.

"It's very foolish I know, bnt I can't help it," he wailed. "I heard Auntie Maud say to granny that she thought I must have forgotten at last, because I laughed so this afternoon. Oh, Aunt Nancy, how can they think such things? I shall *never*, never forget her, and never, never be happy without her!"

"What geese they are!" said Nancy, indignantly. "Maud and Flo don't seem to understand real sorrow a bit. I think I do a little, Mike—I mean I know how awfully you miss her, and how angry you must feel when you think of Edward, and how disgusting everything seems to you here. Oh, dear Mike, if you could but confide in me a little, when you are very miserable indeed! Just talk to me as you would have done to her. I should think it so delicious! Of course, I know that I could never be anything like her to you, but it might do you a little good sometimes to talk things out to some one. I

6—2

know I like to talk things out to Miss May! When one
feels all full to the brim of wretchedness, it's nice to have
somebody to pour it out to, somebody who won't tell you
it's all your own fault and that sort of thing. What *shall*
I do when Miss May's gone!"

"I think we both forget there's God," said Mike,
solemnly, after a pause. "*She* never did it, that's why
He wanted to have her in Heaven, perhaps. But then He
wanted Sprat, too, who wasn't very good. Oh, I can't make
it out! Things are so hard to make out. But you and I
will help each other, Auntie Nancy. I love you very
much."

He threw his arms round her neck. The moon peeped
into the tiny room, and saw them hugging each other.
Out of that hug grew a friendship between the aunt and
nephew which lasted all their lives.

CHAPTER XIII.

WHEN there was any important question to be decided, on which opinions were sure to differ widely, the Hayworths had what they called "conclaves." They shut themselves up in the schoolroom, somebody took the chair, and the subject, whatever it might be, was solemnly discussed.

George, Maud, and Flo did not come to these meetings, but the General, who had instituted them, did occasionally.

He was fond of nipping disputes in the bud by saying— "Summon a conclave, or shut up."

General Hayworth was wise. The members of large families are given to talking at once; they seem to think if they don't there is no chance of having their say, and then they all wish their say to be heard; so to speak the loudest becomes a matter of emulation.

There ought to be a diversity of opinion. It would be tame indeed if a whole pack of brothers and sisters were all of one mind on every topic under the sun. A succession of copies of one set of ideas, however excellent those ideas may be, is as uninteresting as it is unnatural. By all means stick to your opinions, if you have got them, only, tolerate and respect other people's. This was General Hayworth's maxim.

85

One pouring wet day there were two subjects to be discussed in conclave—the puppy's name, and Miss May's parting present. On account of the latter, Miss May was to be excluded from the debate.

"Mamma, please take Miss May to the drawing-room, and have very important things to talk to her about till quarter to four," Nancy whispered to her mother at luncheon.

"And what are the important things to be, Nan—your misdemeanours?" asked Mrs. Hayworth, smiling.

"Yes, if you like," Nancy replied rather flippantly. "Miss May caught me up the chestnut-tree yesterday, and insisted on my descending that instant. I saw old Tabby coming along in her bath-chair, and tried by gesticulating and grimacing to make Miss May see her too, but she wouldn't understand; so I had to climb down. Tabby heard the branches rustling as she passed, and looked up. Of course she caught me in a most 'unladylike position. Oh, how shocked she looked, didn't she, Mike? She told the man to wheel her out of the square directly, and I am sure she called at Miss James's and Miss Smith's on her way home, to describe the disgraceful scene. Now, mamma, dear, you and Miss May, I daresay, can shake your heads over that for an hour or two at least."

"Hush, Nancy, you have rattled on quite long enough," said Mrs. Hayworth, hardly reprovingly, because she made little effort to conceal her amusement.

"I should be ashamed, instead of proud, of being such a tomboy, if I were you," Maud said stiffly. "When I was your age I should never have thought of climbing trees in a public square. No wonder people are shocked."

"Yes, indeed," chimed in Florence. "When you were a small child it didn't matter so much, but now you are much too old to be such a dreadful hoyden."

A warning glance from Miss May arrested the sharp retort on Nancy's lips.

"What hot water I shall get into when she's not there to look at me like that," groaned Nancy inwardly.

Hal, who had been elected president of the conclaves being of a very peace-making disposition, took the chair at two o'clock.

"Dear brethren," he began—"I beg your pardon, I mean, dear ladies and gentlemen—(loud derisive laughter) —we are lucky enough to have come into possession lately of a very fine St. Bernard puppy. Now, this dog as yet does not rejoice in a name. I think we are all decided that he must have a name—('of course !')—but what the name shall be is a matter of great controversy—(a cry of 'Rupert,' followed by "What a donkey you are, Rosey, to interrupt !') Various names have been suggested. I have a list of them here, I think—(a long pause while the president fumbled in his pockets, and, after disclosing their mysteries, brought forth a crumpled piece of paper); out of this list I will read the favourites; then each member will be requested to write on a slip of paper which of them he prefers."

The favourites were Rajah, Scamp, Colin, and Curly.

Charlie then rose and said that he thought Rajah a most suitable name, and that he hoped every one would consider before he voted that the General had wished for it. Nancy was sure the General had said he did not mind whether the dog was called Rajah or Colin. Rosey rattled her bangles in great excitement, and declared that she wouldn't vote for Rajah or Colin, or any name but Rupert. However, the president prevailed on her to reconsider her decision.

The votes were taken, and the majority of them were cast in favour of Rajah. Charlie threw up one of the school-room windows which looked out on the back garden. Jack was there, in spite of rain, busily repairing the damage the puppy had done to the borders by converting them into graves for his bones.

"Jack," shouted Charlie, "the puppy is to be called Rajah, this day, henceforth, and for ever."

"Order," the president demanded. "The business of this afternoon is not over. We have now to talk about a wedding present for a lady. Any one who has any suggestion to make upon this matter is requested to do so, but not at any great length, as I and my friend there have an appointment at four (the appointment was afternoon school), and must leave here at twenty or a quarter to."

Rosey was about to rise, but Nancy held her down unceremoniously, and got up herself.

"That's not fair, is it, Hal?" asked Rosey, querulously. "Why shouldn't I speak first—I am the eldest?"

"That's nothing to do with it. You are so unreasonable, Rosey," said Charlie. " You ought to know by this time that if two people get up together, one must give way."

"But she held me down. It's always the way. You put Nancy before me in everything. It's most unfair, and I shall give Miss May a present all by myself, and not club together." And Rosey relapsed into an injured silence.

Mike, who had been sitting next to Nancy, as quiet as any mouse, during the proceedings, felt sorry for her.

"Let her speak first, Auntie Nancy," he whispered, pulling her dress.

Nancy hesitated for a moment; then said, sitting down again—

"Fire away, Rosey; I'll wait."

Now followed a long enumeration of articles that were "all" not very dear, and "just what Miss May wanted," and "quite lovely."

The assembly took no pains to hide its impatience, and very audibly whispered complaints went round about Rosey's unpractical suggestions. When she resumed her seat, the president said he did not consider any of the fantastical gimcracks the last speaker had praised so rapturously would be useful to a lady going out to Canada, and he hoped something more sensible might be proposed by the next person who spoke. Nancy's mind was divided between a fitted-up travelling-bag and a fur-lined cloak.

These were objected to on the grounds that larger sums of money would be required to buy them than could possibly be collected.

"I always supposed," said Nancy, waxing eloquent, "that everyone was willing to give their last farthing towards this object. Of course, if people don't give liberally, we shall not be able to carry out our plan of presenting Miss May with some really worthy token of our gratitude for all she has done for us. I intend to draw out quite three-quarters of the money I have in the savings-bank, and I hope everyone else will do the same."

There were some rather blank faces at this announcement. Billy, whose deposits in the savings bank were rather few and far between, was very perturbed at being expected to give three-quarters of them towards purchasing such a highly uninteresting thing (to his mind) as a fur-cloak.

"I don't mind subscribing," he spluttered; "but I do think it's throwing away tin to go and give such a lot for an old cloak!"

"Hear, hear, Billy!" exclaimed Charles. "You and I, old boy, will give her the contents of a confectioner's shop. That'll be something like a present, won't it?"

The president hoped there might be no "humbugging," and moved the adjournment of the meeting.

It was proposed that subscriptions should be collected, and then another meeting held to settle what should be done with them. It ended in Miss May getting the fur-lined cloak.

One night, shortly before her departure, when she went into her room, she found it hanging behind the door. It was a beautiful cloak, lined with soft, fluffy, grey squirrel. A piece of paper was pinned to the hood, on which were inscribed the signatures of the donors, and in a bold, familiar handwriting—"To keep our dear Miss May warm when she is skating and sleighing in Canada, and to remind her of her old friends in England."

The governess, proud and pleased as she was with her present, could not help weeping over it.

"Oh, you dears!" she murmured, kissing the scrawl. "How kind, how good and generous of you! As if I should need to be reminded of you! How shall I ever be able to say good-bye to you, I wonder!"

She put on her dressing-gown, and went softly into the next room, where Nancy and Kathy slept. She did this nearly every night, and generally found both asleep. To-night Kathy was as sound as a top, but Nancy only just dozing off, for she had been trying hard to keep awake till Miss May came upstairs. Miss May bent over her and kissed her, and was moving away again, when she leapt up in bed, and, shaking off her drowsiness, said—

"Don't go away. I am awake. Do you like it, Miss May?"

"It's beautiful, dear—far too good for me. I don't deserve such a present, Nancy darling."

"Miss May, you deserve to be as rich as Crœsus! Sit down on the bed, please, and put the candle on the chair, and we'll have a nice little chat. You needn't be afraid

of Kathy waking. I believe if I were to sit on her face
and play the banjo she wouldn't stir."

Nancy, sitting up in her little white bed, with flushed
cheeks, bright eyes, and rough hair, was a pleasant picture.

"A picture I shall have few more chances of looking
at," Miss May said to herself, giving in to Nancy's entreaty,
and sinking down on the end of the bed.

"When I am grown up, Miss May, Mike and I will
come and see you. You know he and I are going round
the world together, and we can easily pay you a visit on
the way. It's the only thing I look forward to being
grown-up for. I don't care a bit about 'coming out.'
The things Maud and Flo like so much I shouldn't care
about at all—going to balls and musical parties, and all
that. I think it must be detestable to be a fashionable
young lady. I hope mother won't try and turn me into one."

"Don't think so much of the future, Nancy. You
know what my favourite poet says:—

> 'Trust no future, howe'er pleasant ;
>   Let the dead past bury its dead.
> Act—act in the living present ;
>   Heart within, and God o'erhead.'

"Yes, Miss May ; but the present without any dreams
and castles in the air is a very dull thing," said Nancy,
sighing heavily. "But I am going to try and see if I
can't make something of it. I should like to teach Jack ;
poor little fellow, he's awfully ignorant; that would be
doing a useful thing, wouldn't it ? If I could only have

all the hours I waste in practising (don't shake your head
Miss May, you know yourself I shall never make anything
of music), I believe I could turn Jack into a scholar in no
time. And then all the money spent on my music lessons!
What lots of good that would do. It would buy a splendid
little livery, with beautiful buttons, for one thing. Oh, I
want to see Jack a regular page so badly. He's quite
sharp enough. Fancy how lovely he'd look in buttons.
There I am, drifting off into the future again, for Jack in
buttons is quite a thing of the future. I say, Miss May,
you will write me letters all to myself, and I shall write
to you and tell you everything. You won't be vexed if
the writing is bad; because I am sure one can't write out
one's whole heart without blots and smudges."

There was silence for a few minutes. Miss May,s heart
was too full for words. She rested her face in her hands,
and prayed that this stormy young soul might not be
baffled with the trials, temptations, and disappointments
that inevitably were in store for it. Then she rose, and
putting her arms round Nancy, whispered—

"God bless you, my child. Life will be a hard battle
for you, but with His help you may came out of it crowned
with laurels."

She took her candle, and giving Kathy another kiss,
left the room.

"That is a grand idea," thought Nancy as she closed
her eyes. "I—Mike and I—will be soldiers in the *battle
of life*. How we will fight!"

CHAPTER XIV.

MIKE GOES TO SCHOOL.

AFTER the Christmas holidays there were some con-
siderable changes made in the family routine. It
was felt that Miss May's place could not be filled. So
Rosey and Nancy were sent to the High School which
had just been started in Halminster, Billy went to the
college with his elder brethren, and a German governess
was coming to undertake Kathy's education. At first it
had been suggested that Mike should be a companion to
Kathy in her studies, but he had implored that he might
be sent to school like Uncle Billy. There was a pre-
paratory establishment in Abercrombie Square, kept by a
Mr. Parkinson, where most of the college boys had begun
school life, and which was called by some of them the
"nursery." Here it was decided Mike should go for a
term, or perhaps longer. He started the first morning
quite alone to face the swarms of small boys whom he
had often seen in the square, after the hours of twelve
and four, skirmishing about, engaged in some inexplicable
games of their own invention, in which a great deal of
punching and yelling seemed absolutely necessary to keep
up the spirit of the thing. Mike was more in awe of
this strange crew than of long-legged Mr. Parkinson, with

94

his heavy dark moustache and kind brown eyes, who was very like a great overgrown boy himself, out of school. In it, he was a very formidable pedagogue indeed, and not at all inclined to look on the application of the cane to small horny palms as an old-fashioned and exploded practice. All the "Parkites" wore dark blue caps with white stars on the crown. Mike's had a small piece of crape sewn to the peak, and this sign of mourning, together with his solemn face, struck the merry little fellows brimming over with spirits and mischief, and they let him off the teasing, pinching, and cross-questioning they generally inflicted on a new boy. He heard one say to another—

"That's the Hayworths' nephew; his mother died a short time ago, and he's awfully cut up."

"Then we won't humbug him," answered the other, a fresh-complexioned boy in velveteen knickerbockers, with a thick shock of fiery red hair and a very wide mouth, which just for a moment stopped grinning, as he reflected how he should feel without a mother at home to get him out of scrapes, to order him good puddings, and to let him have friends to tea, and to do a great many other things with which a mother was associated in his mind. "Carrots," however, was not given to sentiment, and soon dispelled uncomfortable thoughts by twitching a cap off a curly head near him, and rushing away with it at full speed, while capless pursued the wrong person.

Mike watched their pranks for a few minutes, then,

after refusing two or three invitations to join in them, went home. Of course his aunts were very anxious to know how he had got on, what class he had been put in, and what lessons he had to do for the next day, and whether he liked his schoolfellows? Indeed every one put a question to Mike at lunch except Nancy. She, who watched him so jealously, saw he would much rather be left in peace.

"How can he possibly know whether he likes them after one morning. Such a ridiculous thing to ask," said Nancy, flashing an angry glance at Maud. "I have been at the High School a week, and I am sure I don't know yet whether I like a single girl there. I do know, though, that I heartily dislike most of them."

"Oh Nancy!" exclaimed Rosey, perking up, "I am sure some of them are very jolly. Fatima Headland is a pet. The first moment I saw her I fell in love with her; and isn't it funny she did with me? Hatty and Mabel Barnes are sweet too, but I shall have Fatima for my chum. She has got the most beautiful auburn hair and hazel eyes. George, you would think her lovely."

"Should I really," said George gruffly. "I don't as a rule admire the people you go into raptures over."

"She isn't very pretty," Nancy said, "and a most awfully cocksy child."

"Child! Really, Nancy, she is at least two years older than you. Please remember she is my very *best* friend, and don't abuse her."

"Stop this wrangling immediately," the General said peremptorily from the other side of the joint, "or I shall refuse to carve for you. I must say," he went on, laughing, "of two evils, I would rather have boys than girls; they do at least keep their tongues still. Billy here is a pattern to you all. He never talks at meals, so manages to eat twice as much as any of you. Look what a fine specimen he is in consequence. Why, he has got more fat on one cheek than that chattering Rose has on her whole body."

In this way General Hayworth, by causing a general laugh, made peace between the belligerents. Mrs. Hayworth played bo-peep behind the plant in the centre of the table, to smile her gratitude at her husband, who purposely put his head the side hers was not. This was a source of further amusement, and everybody when they rose from the table was in a good humour.

Mike soon got used to school, and took a great interest in his work. He was moved two classes higher than the one he had been placed in at first, for it was found he was quite capable of working with boys much older than himself.

Mr. Parkinson stopped the General one day in the square, and told him his grandson was surprisingly indus- trious and intelligent, but not in the least priggish, like the clever lads sometimes were.

"A prig—no, indeed! My Violet took pretty good care he should not be that," answered General Hayworth,

7

huskily.   His voice always lost its cheerful ring when he spoke of her who was gone, the eldest and best beloved of his flock.

"Old Parky has been cracking up Mike to the pater," remarked Charlie, dragging a chair to the school-room table, and beginning to scribble what he called an "im-pot" over a sheet of foolscap paper.   "I think myself it was rather a mistake not to send him to the college and Billy to the 'nursery.'   Our William seems to find the bottom of the second a very comfortable seat!   I rather wonder if he'll ever get any higher."

Billy hid his confusion by standing on his head in the decrepit leather arm-chair, a proceeding which astonished no one, as it was a very favourite position of his, and one in which he was constantly seen.   In fact, Billy was as much at home on his head as most people are on their feet.   He was very glad of the refuge now.   Disparaging as Charlie's remark was, his boots couldn't blush, and his burning face was safely concealed in the recesses of the old chair.

Mike lifted his great eyes from a Latin exercise, and said, much distressed—

"Oh, no, Uncle Charlie; I should have been much too backward for the college.   I can't do arithmetic a bit, and Uncle Billy is awfully good at it."

The muddy boots slowly descended from mid-air, and Billy's large, black, curly head resumed its normal position.

"What's your 'swot' to-night?" he inquired of Mike,

looking over his shoulder. "If you have any sums to do, I'll help you work them."

"Oh, thank you so much! How jolly of you!" said Mike, eagerly responding to the recognition of his little compliment. "I have just two more sentences of this exercise to do, and then I will begin my sums."

"You had better be doing your own work, Billy," said Charlie, who had by this time covered another sheet of foolscap, and clothed his second finger down to the third joint with ink. "Hang old Judy! What system of education he wants to carry out by giving a fellow an imposition every day I can't conceive."

"Hal never gets any," said Rosey; "so it shows it must be your own fault."

"Wait till Hal is in Judy's form, then we shall see."

It was extraordinary how Charlie's tongue could keep pace with his pen ; he hardly ever stopped talking while he wrote.

Hal, on the contrary, even when his own name was mentioned, maintained complete silence, and he hardly raised his head from his books when Nancy entered the room like a whirlwind, scattering pens, pencils, and papers all round her.

"I say, Mike, George says you and I may do our work in his study. Isn't it jolly of him ? He's going out this evening, and we may stay there till your bed-time," she said in high glee.

"Dear me ! is that all ? One would have thought the

7—2

house was on fire from the way you rushed into the room," Rosey said, rather crossly. "You have driven that word out of my head, and I shall have to look it out again. This translation is much more difficult than any Miss May ever gave us to do."

"Come along, Mike. Let's get out of this hubbub."

"That is good, Nancy," said Charlie. "You, the very incarnation of noisiness, come and disturb us, quiet studious people, and then say, 'Let's get out of the hubbub!'"

"I have done all my lessons, Aunt Nancy, except my sums, and Uncle Billy is going to help me with them."

"Done! Why, I haven't even begun. I have been teaching Rajah to catch biscuit, and never knew how time was going. Well, come to the study when you've finished." And Nancy vanished.

Mike did not go as soon as he might have done, for he knew what a quantity of work Nancy had before her, and thought it as well to leave her at least half an hour to herself.

When the books were strapped up, and Charlie and Hal had sat down to a game of chess, and Rosey had gone to adorn herself for a half-hour in the drawing-room before bed-time, Mike slipped into the study.

It was a room about the size of a silk pocket-handkerchief, in the fitting up of which George had displayed much decorative talent. The walls were hung with pictures and a great many other things, such as Indian shoes, old-fashioned daggers, skulls, epaulets, helmets, quaint

fishing-tackle, delightfully hideous Chinese idols, etc.
There was a small table and carved chair in the window,
and here the few things that denoted study were crowded.
The glory of the apartment was a noble tiger-skin spread
on the stained floor, which the General always declared
George had filched from him by main force. On this
Nancy was stretched at full length in the same position of
the "Reading Girl," quite too engrossed in a book to notice
the entrance of her nephew. It couldn't be a lesson-book,
or she would not be so intent, he thought.

"Nancy"—(when they were alone Mike sometimes
dropped the "Aunt")—"you surely have begun your
lessons?"

Nancy gave herself a luxurious roll in the tiger-skin.

"Mike, have you ever read 'Westward Ho!' If you
have, you can imagine what my disgust is at being reminded of such odious things as lessons just in the middle
of the part where they landed, and grabbed the prickly
pears and purple grapes, and the old crabs looked out of
their holes at them. Oh, Mike, it's horrid to think there
is no new country to be discovered now. Nothing is
unknown now, but the old North Pole, which I believe
is only a field of ice." And Nancy began to give Mike
a glowing, vivid epitome of what she had been reading—
indeed of the whole book; for she had read it over and
over again, and knew it nearly by heart. Nancy had a
gallery of heroes, but the fair-haired giant, Sir Amyas
Legh, for the present towered above them all.

The boy was enchanted. He knelt on the tiger-skin with shining wide eyes and parted lips, drinking it all in eagerly. His spirit soared away out of his little nineteenth-century mourning suit, back across the ages to that glorious time of heroic enterprise and loyal emotion, when the brave young men of Devon went forth to wrest a golden world from the Spaniard for their queen and country.

"How splendidly they did their duty!" he exclaimed.

"Yes, but what a glorious duty it was; how different to ours!" said Nancy. "I haven't done mine to-day; indeed, Mike, I haven't been keeping my resolution to fight my faults." She got up quickly from the seductive skin and gave it a petulant kick. "I shall never win any victories at this rate. To begin with this morning, I didn't get up when Hester called us. The night had seemed only a minute; so I indulged in a conscious snooze till Kathy was dressed. When I floundered out of bed I was angry with myself for having done it. I thought I should be late, so scurried into my bath and dashed the water about in a rage, and didn't fold up my night-dress or say my prayers. Then I shook Kathy because she had taken my gloves instead of her own, and I couldn't find them anywhere; and I quarrelled with Rosey all the way to school, and I was snappish to dear old Hal at tea; and now I have dawdled away the whole evening in amusing myself. Oh, if when my eye fell on 'Westward Ho!' I had only made an attempt to fight down the longing to peep into it! I have often heard papa say that lazy, self-indulgent people, who can't deny themselves things they like, are not fit to be soldiers. And that is just what I am. You get on splendidly, Mike; you never seem to have any trouble in doing your duty. I believe the fact is, you have no faults at all!"

The lines about Mike's firm mouth became hard; he clutched Nancy's hand, and said, in a voice strangely unlike his usual gentle tones, "I have hundreds of faults; and if I hadn't, I have got one giant sin which is enough to make me wicked without them."

"Why, Mike, what is that?" asked Nancy.

"I can't forgive father! I stop in my prayers at the place where I used to ask God to bless him. I feel as if I couldn't mention him without being a hypocrite. Oh, it is such an awful feeling! But I can't help it. When I think how he used to talk of taking me to Rome, and all the great places, and speak to me as if I was quite grown up, and then, just when I wanted him so much, to treat me in that cruel way! I wouldn't have minded if he had beaten me, if he had only seemed like a father and let me live with him. But I know I ought to love him just the same, and that's why I am wicked, because sometimes I feel as if I almost hated him!"

"I have felt so too; but, then, he is not my father. Yes, Mike, I suppose it must be very wrong. Make war on the giant! Begin a campaign this very night, and fight and fight at him till you take him prisoner, and then you will be able to kill him fast enough. I declare there's the porridge going into the school-room; I hear the plates rattling. We must go down and say good-night. Mamma will sure to be vexed that I didn't go down with Rosey; and I sha'n't be able to say I was too busy, for I have done simply nothing. So ends this horrid day! I am determined to-morrow shall be better."

The drawing-room was a handsome, luxurious room, filled with all kinds of Indian treasures. Maud and Flo looked very pretty in their picturesque evening dresses, one seated at the piano and the other making tea; and as to General and Mrs. Hayworth, a finer looking couple than they never sat at a backgammon board together! They all looked nice, even Rosey, Nancy thought, as she and Mike came across the soft carpet, blinking their eyes at the brilliant lights, which were dazzling—after the one dim lamp in George's study.

"Well, my boy," said the General, lifting Mike on his knee, "I have seen precious little of you to-day. That tomboy aunt of yours monopolizes you entirely!"

"She is very good to me, grandpapa," he said, leaning his head against General Hayworth's broad shoulders. He had been reading about the Indian Mutiny in the history class at Mr. Parkinson's, and was proud to nestle against the great chest of one of the bravest of the many gallant officers that took part in that awful fray.

"My dear child, how untidy you are!" exclaimed Mrs.

Hayworth, looking in dismay at Nancy's torn black frock, crumpled brown holland apron, and wild hair.

"It was not worth while making one's self respectable just to come and say good-night, mother dear. I am sorry I kept Mike up so late, but without Miss May to remind me, I never know the time!"

"Well, you will have Fräulein Walder here soon, and then I hope you will get into better ways again."

Nancy shrugged her shoulders. She was not looking forward to the advent of the new governess with any satisfaction.

"If Rosey can get her lessons done in good time, I see no reason why Nancy should not," said Flo, dropping sugar into pretty little white cups with butterfly handles, which she had painted herself.

"I have not been doing them all this time," said Nancy, honestly. "I shall have to get up at half-past five to-morrow. Yes, I know I deserve a scolding, mother, so please give it to me."

It was Maud and Florence who remonstrated, however, and not Mrs. Hayworth. They held up Rosey as an example, and that little person's undisguised satisfaction, as she sat on a small chair copying a pattern of her darling Fatima Headland's, in crewel work, was very exasperating to Nancy; but she bit her lips, and made no sharp remark, only told Rosey supper was ready, and then after saying "good-night" all round, she and Mike departed.

"Those two are devoted friends," said Mrs. Hayworth when they were gone.

"Yes," chirped Rosey, "and they have such funny conversations together, you can't think. They call themselves soldiers, and I don't know what else. They said doing anything you don't like is winning a victory. It is a secret between them, so I suppose I oughtn't to tell any more."

"Certainly not," said the General, shortly. "Goodnight, my dear."

Rosey gathered up her crewels, and took her father's hint, feeling rather snubbed. She enjoyed entertaining her sisters with school gossip, and when that was exhausted, very, often, I am sorry to say, regaled them with stories of Nancy and Mike, or Billy and Kathy. Perhaps this was the reason she had lately become a great favourite with her elders, who pronounced her "a very amusing little thing." They were rather afraid to patronize Nancy. She puzzled them. She was so childish in her ways, and so strangely old in her thoughts. Full of incongruities and startling ideas, her character was a riddle to them, although they would not have owned it for the world.

Poor Nancy, vastly inferior as she might be in many respects to those two tall, fair-haired, perfectly correct elder sisters of hers, yet she was in possession of a few things which they had not; a large sympathetic young heart, and, above all, a knowledge of the grand significance of duty.

CHAPTER XV.

NATURALLY the children speculated a good deal on the appearance, temper, and qualities in general of the new governess. Nancy had made up her mind, although her mother had told her she was quite young, that she would be a severe old dowdy with spectacles like the Fräulein who used to bring a party of young ladies to Mr. Daintytop's dancing class, and sit bolt upright on a form knitting and glaring in a most forbidding way at the feet of her charges as they laboured through the intricate mazes of Polish mazurkas, gavottes, and minuets. By this solitary specimen Nancy judged all German governesses and spinsters. Rosey had a more romantic notion. She had seen a picture of Gretchen in an *edition de luxe* of selections from "Faust," and fondly hoped the new governess would resemble it, at any rate as far as the long plaits of hair were concerned. Kathy was convinced she would turn out a perfect Tartar, and was determined to meet her as a personal enemy; she had been having rather an easy time of it since Miss May's departure, only getting some intermittent and listless instruction from her elder sisters, which suited her tastes admirably. Kathy was decidedly lazy.

"She will be very sour," Hal said; "for of course she
has lived on sauerkraut all her life."

"And sausage too.   She's a saucy girl if she eats
saus-age," said Charlie, taking precautions as he spoke to
shield himself from the attacks such an execrable pun was
likely to provoke.

"Whatever she is like, I shall not care for her.
Besides, there is no reason why anyone but Kathy should
like her; we shall not have much to do with her."

"Indeed, Nancy, we are to obey her and go out walks
with her and all that.   If she is nice, I shall rather like
it," said Rosey.

"Oh yes; I daresay you will.   I quite expect to see
you bosom friends with her before long.   We shall no
doubt hear soon that Miss May was no loss," replied
Nancy, in hot scorn.   She thought it an insult to Miss
May's memory to have the smallest regard for her
successor.

Poor little Fräulein!   She came straight from her picturesque German home with a determination to love and
be loved by the little "Engländers," and she was rather
chilled by her reception.   They made her no advances,
and took no pains to understand her broken English.
Her first day was Sunday.   She came down ready for
church in a neatly fitting grey dress, which was rather
spoilt by an elaborate blue bow and wide embroidered
collar, but this arrangement nevertheless became her
blooming complexion.   She was not at all the bony, for-

bidding old maid Nancy had expected. Nor was she the slim beautiful maiden of Rosey's fancy. She was just a fresh, simple little Teuton, with a round figure and a mass of light brown hair, which could not possibly have been squeezed into a fashionable English knot, and her small blue eyes looked straight at you in a very honest fashion. She felt home-sick and lonely, tucked in at the end of the long cathedral pew, which, roomy as it was, did not hold all the Hayworths. The service of course was strange to her, and she fluttered the leaves of a prayer book in utter bewilderment, looking helplessly now and then at her neighbour Kathy, who kept her eyes resolutely on her book; next to her came Nancy and Rosey, and then George. He, by dint of nudges and frowns, hinted to Nancy that she might offer to find the psalms for Fräulein. Now among our heroine's numerous failings, she had one which constantly brought her into trouble; this was an utter inability to control her laughter when anything amused her. Something in George's face struck her as comical, she smiled, and then from sheer nervousness of doing such a dreadful thing as laugh in church, made some extraordinary phizzing sounds which reminded the boys of ginger-beer bottles going off, and made Billy, who was sitting in front, screw his head round, and look over the starchiest of Eton collars with watering lips. Fräulein concluded that she must be the cause of this unseemly mirth. "How unkind and unmannerly," she thought, the blood rising to her brow, and the tears to her eyes; "how

can I know their ways so soon? Ah, we do not treat
foreigners like that when they come to our churches; and
how wicked, too, to make jokes in a holy place." George
thrust his arm impatiently over his three sisters, and
handed her his prayer-book. "What a caddish thing to
laugh at a foreigner," he whispered to Nancy, accompanying
the remark with a vehement pressure of her ten toes.
This timely torture prevented another explosion, and
brought forth the loudly whispered, indignant protest——

"I was not laughing at *her*, as *if* I should."

Both Maud and Florence cast withering glances at the
delinquent, and General Hayworth looked terribly severe.
Nancy heartily wished that the prayers and litany came
before the first lesson, that she might kneel down and
bury her confusion.

Nancy always walked home from church with her
father. He liked a strong young arm to lean on, for
sharp attacks of gout had lamed him considerably. How
supremely proud and happy she was to be his staff, I
cannot say. She wasn't even jealous on this occasion if
Mike walked with Rosey. She loved to stand by her
father as he spoke to the people he knew coming out of
church. They all seemed so pleased with his cordial
greeting. Canon Brown's old sisters flushed up to the
roots of their auburn fronts, and fluttered their lavender
bonnet strings at his gallant speeches. He chaffed the
prim little Fosters till they were positively compelled to
laugh, and made fat little Dr. Headland forget he was so

close to the church door and roar at his jokes. He had a cheery word for old and young alike, and the most crabbed and sour could not resist him. Nancy often thought that girls who had little, stumpy, purple-faced men for fathers like Fatima Headland, or wizened up bookworms like Jane and Alice Forster, must envy her hers, with his fine military figure and splendid Roman nose.

To-day, as they walked along under the lime trees in the Cathedral Green, Nancy knew her father was meditating a lecture, for he looked grave and had not made one remark since they parted from the Misses Brown at the end of the walk.

"Nancy," he said at last, "I should advise you not to have Jack up this afternoon."

"Why not, papa!"

"Because, my dear, it is evident you have no self-control. People who haven't should never attempt to rule or teach others."

"Oh, I did try hard not to laugh. Really, papa, I think it is a disease I have got. If anything tickles me in the very least, I feel a kind of weak feeling inside, and then I must laugh, or if I bottle it in, make those dreadful noises. I can't help it."

"If you can't help giggling I am extremely sorry, for there is no habit more intolerable."

Nancy said no more. She was very much ashamed of herself.

CHAPTER XVI.

GEORGE INTERFERES.

AFTER dinner Nancy said to Mike, "Will you read to Jack this afternoon? I am not fit for it. It is a pity he should be disappointed; he does like it so."

"Oh, Aunt Nancy," Mike exclaimed, looking rather alarmed; "I don't think Jack would care for me to read to him. You see I am younger than he is, and I can't explain things like you do. What do you mean about not being fit for it? You teach him splendidly!"

"Oh, no, I don't. It's all the night-school. Papa says I am not fit to teach any one, and he is right. Why did I behave in that utterly foolish way? I do despise myself for it now. But that face of George's is always too much for me." And Nancy began to smile even in the midst of her humiliation and distress.

They were sitting together in a low window-seat at the end of one of the long passages. There were many private nooks such as this in the old house, which made it a convenient one for parties. Many a flirtation had been carried on in this retired corner, where the youthful aunt and nephew often resorted to have talks too confidential for the publicity of the schoolroom.

"I remember Flo sitting here with Phil Travers once

112

under a Chinese lantern for such a time. Rosey and I were peeping over the stairs. We don't have dances now, and I am glad of it," said Nancy, looking at her black frock. "I wish we could stay in mourning for ever. The very sound of the 'Sweethearts' Waltz' made me think of Mr. Daintytop, and the very thought of Mr. Daintytop used to give me the nightmare. Ah, Mike, you may be thankful you never had to go to the dancing-class! I expect you would have, if Miss May had not gone away. Billy used to go. But I wouldn't mind enduring even a dancing lesson every day, if I could have my dear darling Miss May back."

Nancy sighed heavily, and then went wandering on again, speaking her thoughts, as she was accustomed to do when she had Mike by her side in what she called a "gossip retreat."

Just now he was not a very attentive listener, and at last interrupted Nancy in the middle of her reflections by saying, "I will read to Jack, if you really won't."

"Oh, thank you, dear; but don't do it if you would rather not."

"I would rather not; but you know, Aunt Nan, it is good drill," answered Mike.

"Yes, of course it is. I will go and get "Ministering Children," and show you where to begin. Just read him a chapter, and hear him his text, and that will do."

Jack was waiting in the breakfast-room, with his hair plastered down, and his face shining like a looking-glass,

8

thumbing a bigly-printed Testament which Nancy had presented to him.

"Master Mike will read to you to-day, Jack," said Nancy, briefly introducing her substitute, and then shutting the door on the two boys without more ado.

Mike felt very shy, and tried to think of something to say, for he thought it wouldn't do to begin to read straight away.

Jack, to his great relief, broke the silence.

"I ain't never forgot that prayer you prayed when Sprat was dyin'. God did what you asked Him, for He took Sprat to Heaven, and I reckon made him well when He got 'm there: and He found me friends, and no mistake. I wish some of the chaps I knowed could hear a prayer like that now and again; it 'ud do 'em a lot of good. I means them that never knew the name of God, except as a cuss. It hain't their fault. Sprat used to swear good 'uns, but he knew no better."

"What a shame it is that every one shouldn't be taught about God!" said Mike, with kindling eyes. Now the ice was broken, he forgot his shyness. "I think when I am a man, and have got a lot of money, I will have a school for all the poor, dirty boys I can find; and I will give them lots of good things to eat, and teach them, and make them happy."

"And Miss Nancy, she'll be a rare one to help you!" Jack said, entering into the philanthropic scheme with eagerness.

"And you shall help me, too, Jack; and I shall try and get Janet to come to mend all their clothes and keep them tidy. I hope she won't have grown too old by that time. For, of course, it will be a *long, long* time before I shall be able to do what I like. Perhaps, after all, it is best not to talk about it, for a great deal may happen before I am a man. Now, Jack, I must read to you, or there will be no time."

So Mike read, and was quite sorry, instead of glad, when the hour was over. Nancy consoled herself by writing a long letter to Miss May, in which she poured out her heart in very black back-handed hieroglyphics. She told her how the new governess had come, and how quite impossible it would be ever to like her in the least bit; how she couldn't bear to see her sitting in Miss May's place at the school-room table, and a great deal more, that was equally unreasonable. It was a pity the letter Miss May wrote in answer to this took such a long time in coming, for in it she strongly expressed her disapproval of Nancy's conduct to Fräulein, and assured her that nothing could grieve her more than that the children should be unkind to their governess, and if they thought it was doing any honour to her, they were mistaken.

Nancy began to see her folly directly it was pointed out to her by Miss May, but I am afraid not before.

However, Fräulein from that first Sunday had one staunch ally in the family, and that was George. He often made some excuse for coming into the school-room

8—2

in the morning, to see how Kathy was behaving herself
When he found her (he generally did) with a sulky,
defiant expression on her face, and something in her
whole bearing very discouraging to her teacher, he would
pretend he could not find the book he had come for, and
linger about looking for it. Kathy had strong suspicions
that he came to spy on her, and one day determined to
maintain a stubborn silence as long as he was in the room.
Fräulein was using all her powers of persuasion to get
some enlightenment on the subject of the war of the
"Spanish Succession;" but in vain! She might as well
have tried to draw blood from a stone as a ray of enthusiasm from Kathy, or the smallest display of patriotic
pride in the mighty victories of the Duke of Marlborough.

"You cannot then have learned the history at all?"
exclaimed poor Fräulein at last in sheer despair.

"I have," muttered Kathy.

"Then surely you know the name of the General who
ordered your forces on that memorable opportunity?"

Fräulein's English was rather ambitious.

"I do know it," persisted Kathy.

"Then tell me, dear."

Dead silence. George could hold out no longer.

"My dear Kath," he said, seating himself on the corner
of the table with his hands in his pockets, and an air of
mock gravity which rather frightened the untractable
pupil. "I am sorry to doubt the truth of your state-
ments, but I think it highly improbable that a little girl

who had prepared a lesson would refuse to answer a single question on it. However, we will take you at your word," he went on, encouraged by seeing he had dispelled the harassed expression from Fräulein's face and made her smile and show her dimples. "You have entirely mastered this interesting period of history. You couldn't be puzzled, you have it all so pat. Then how are we to account for your extraordinary conduct? If it is not ignorance it must be temper. I am sorry to see that my youngest sister is developing a *bad temper*."

Having finished this impressive oration, George looked at his watch, which reminded him it was time to go to his tutor's.

"Now, Kathy, that sour face of yours will become stationary if you don't look out. It'll be bad enough to be an ignoramus when you are grown up, without being a shrew into the bargain. To look at you one would think you had a dragon to teach you instead of . . . . " The door had to be opened at this point, and George finished his sentence the other side of it.

"George, what have you been doing in the school-room? You will be late at Dr. Buzfeld's," called Flo from the breakfast-room, as he went whistling down the stairs.

"They treat that poor little German abominably," he growled, and went his way.

It soon was an acknowledged thing that George was Fräulein's champion. The other boys, too, declared her to be "not half bad," and only the girls remained obdurate and persisted in their cold indifferent manner towards her. Nancy because she had made up her mind not to make a friend of her, Rosey because she was afraid of Nancy's wrath and contempt, and being called untrue to Miss May, and Kathy out of sheer naughtiness.

"What do you think, Fräulein's crying!"

This announcement was made by Rosey one morning early in the Easter holidays, when the luxury of doing nothing had not yet become wearisome; at least, every one in the schoolroom seemed to be enjoying it to the full.

"I wonder she isn't rejoicing, not lamenting, at being let off the drudgery of hammering 'der, die, das,' into the thick head of my sister Katharine," said Charlie. "I say, Kath, do you know the German yet for 'The sister of my father has given the hat of my brother to the neighbour of thy uncle'?"

Kathy was far too pleasantly engaged in eating an orange to be much disturbed at this reminder of Otto's grammar; she only gave her quizzing brother a withering glance, and sucked her orange more vigorously than ever.

"What can she be crying for, Nancy?" Rosey went on. "The door between our room and hers was open, so I could hear her sobbing quite plainly. I really felt sorry for her."

"Weak-minded, sentimental people often shed tears to excite interest," said Nancy, cuttingly. "I beg your pardon, Hal," she added, as a pair of flashing brown eyes met hers. "I forgot you were one of the true knights of the Jungfrau."

"I wouldn't try to be sarcastic if I were you. It isn't in your *rôle* at all," said Hal. "Any fellow would be struck with the way you treat Fräulein. If she were a horrid old blue-stocking instead of a jolly, pleasant sort of girl, I should think it a shame, but more excusable. I heard the mater jawing her because she didn't talk German enough to you. A lot of encouragement you give her to talk German, or any other civilized language. I should like to see you or Rosey shipped off somewhere. I wonder how you would get on as governesses. I expect you'd both yell with home-sickness before you had been gone an hour."

"Hear, hear, Hal!" cried Charlie. "You and George will be having a duel soon. I'll be his second, and Harding will be yours, won't you, old fellow?"

Harding was as much at home at the Hayworths as he was under the paternal roof, and spent a great deal of his time there in the holidays. He was at present ensconced in the veteran arm-chair, with Hal perched on one arm and Charlie on the other. Every now and then there was a great lurch, and the long-suffering article of furniture creaked ominously, and threatened to succumb altogether. Poor old chair! Like all of us it had been young once. There had been a time, although it was hard to believe it, when it possessed springs, and looked glossy and plump, and ready to burst with pride in its polished brass nails, and sturdy spread-out legs! Now in its crabbed old age youth bumped and battered it, and showed it not the smallest degree of respect! No wonder it wore an injured air, and groaned sulkily when any one sat down on it.

The subject of conversation came into the room before Harding had time to answer. There certainly were traces of tears on her face, but she was making a struggle to look her bright self again. She timidly proposed a walk. Nancy shrugged her shoulders, and murmured something about rain, without looking up from her book. But Rosey, who was very fond of sifting things, wanted to find out the cause of Fräulein's tears, and said she thought the best thing they could do would be to go for a walk.

"Come, Billy and Kathy, you must go whether you like it or not, if Fräulein says so," she said, turning to the twins.

Kathy had squeezed her orange dry by this time.

"You see it lasts much longer if you eat it that way, Billy. If you peel it like you did yours, and make it into quarters, it's all gone in a minute."

"I don't care about its lasting, as long as I don't waste any."

"Oh, you pair of gourmandizers! You had decidedly better go out, or you won't be able to get up an appetite for dinner," cried Charlie.

Billy felt rather mortified at being expected to go out with a governess now he was a college boy.

"I suppose I shall be treated as part of Kathy all my life," he thought. "I wish I had never been born a twin!"

CHAPTER XVII.

FRÄULEIN'S BIRTHDAY.

NANCY was determined to stay at home. Mike had gone out with his grandfather, and without his company or Rajah's, who had gone too, a walk would be intolerable. Rosey was glad she didn't come, for she was able to take Fräulein's arm, and make other friendly overtures, which she would have been rather afraid to do in Nancy's presence.

Fräulein was pleased, and warmed up at the unwonted attention, and was not at all unwilling to tell why she had been crying when Rosey hinted she wanted to know. She knew it was foolish, but she had felt very wretched that morning because it was her birthday. Birthdays were great days in her country, even when you were grown up. Hers always was such a happy one, and she couldn't help thinking to-day how she had spent it last year, although she knew she shouldn't think of it, for it gave her dreadful "Heimweh." Then she told them about the festivities and simple pleasures of a German birthday. The little table covered with a spotless white cloth, and decorated with flowers, on which all kinds of presents were arranged. The beautiful cake in the middle. Then the excursion to the woods, where the Birthday Queen was crowned, and in the evening the health-drinking and the cotillion and polonaise. Oh! one had a merry time of it on one's birthday in the dear old fatherland.

"And not one of us has even wished you many happy returns of the day. It does seem too bad," said Rosey. "I wish I had asked you to write your name in my Shakespeare birthday-book, and then I should have known."

"What sort of cakes do you have in Germany?" asked Kathy.

"Oh, such pretty ones. There are many kinds, but on birthdays we have the most beautiful that can be made; at least we do at home."

"As good as wedding-cake?" Billy inquired, all at once becoming deeply interested in the conversation.

"I never tasted your wedding-cake," said Fräulein. "It looks so very black and solid, I do not think it would be nice."

"But don't you Germans have wedding-cakes?" exclaimed Billy, opening his eyes very wide, and looking as if he thought it wouldn't be much fun to be married without the important item.

"*Gewiss!* But ours are quite different. Not black at all; they are very tall and white, and more delicate to look at than yours."

"Nothing can beat ours!" said Billy, who thought wedding-cake the most delicious ambrosia, and only wished he could have the chance of "tucking in" to it well, instead of only getting a crumb now and then.

"I remember when Nancy and I were bridesmaids to Vi, we were allowed to eat as much cake as we liked. Billy, you would have enjoyed it, wouldn't you?" said Rosey.

"You did, too, I expect, although you talk as if you were above it," Billy replied. Then, looking compassion. ately at Fräulein, he added, "No wonder you cried; fancy a birthday with no cake, and no tips, and no anything!"

Fräulein wished them to understand that she hadn't been lamenting over the absence of cakes and presents; but it was the thought of spending a birthday for the first time in her life without her dear ones made her feel so sad. Then she told them about her sister Theresa, her tall soldier brother Max, and Gretchen, with her golden pig-tails, and baby Fritz, and a great deal about her home, which even Kathy was obliged to own was very enter-taining.

When they got home after their walk, Rosey boldly de-clared before Nancy that Fräulein was a "dear little thing."

Nancy looked at her with a contemptuous "I-thought-as-much" air, which did not concern Rosey in the least, for she felt that she had nearly the whole family to back her up in her opinion. Even Maud and Florence had patronized Fräulein lately, and talked of reading "Wallenstein" with her, by way of improving their German.

That afternoon all the school-room party received a very imposing invitation card—

"Mr. GEORGE HAYWORTH,
At Home,
5 till 9.
To meet Fräulein Walder.
"An immediate answer is requested."

"Oh, what fun!" exclaimed Rosey.

"Shall we all be able to cram into the study?" inquired wise Mike.

"It will be rather a tight fit.   But it can be managed," said Hal.   He and Charlie had been taken into George's confidence.   One had helped to print the cards, and the other had gone out and come in laden with bulky paper bags of "tuck," the sight of which would have made Billy's heart beat a little faster.

Nancy, when she first pulled her card out of the envelope, had laughed as much and looked as pleased as the others; but soon her silly prejudice got the mastery of her again.

"George never troubled himself about Miss May's birthday, and she had known us all our lives," she said.

"If George didn't, every one else did," replied Hal. "Besides, how can it hurt Miss May if we are civil to Fräulein?   She would be the last to encourage such a stupid notion."

Nancy did not answer, but flipped her invitation card into the grate with very badly-assumed indifference, for she had an uncomfortable conviction that every one would think her extremely disagreeable.

"That means you don't intend to come, I suppose," said Hal, indignantly. "Very well, stay away; there will be more room for other people."

"Oh, no! Aunt Nancy must come," exclaimed Mike, who had got out his desk to answer the invitation. "It won't be fun without her."

But Aunt Nancy didn't go, and it *was* great fun, in spite of that. Only one person could not get over her absence, and that was Mike. He had tried hard to persuade her to come up to the last moment, but she obstinately refused.

The feast was most ingeniously arranged on various small tables, as it was impossible to get a fair-sized one into the room. Fräulein was given the carved oak-chair as the seat of honour; she was conducted to it by George as if she had been the Queen; Charlie and Hal superintended the packing in of the rest, and when this by-no-means easy task was accomplished the door was closed and the business began.

The General had been invited, but, rather to the relief of the host, had declined. Where his huge limbs would have been stowed, if he had come, is a problem I cannot pretend to solve. George had to keep his long legs doubled up, or he certainly would have kicked his principal guest, which would never have done. Perhaps the chief feature of the entertainment was Jack arrayed in a gorgeous

Indian costume, with his face and hands blacked. This was Charlie's idea, who thought it would add to the picturesqueness of the affair to have such a resplendent waiter. Unfortunately, space would not allow of Jack's doing anything in the waiting line, and he was obliged to stand perched on a footstool in a very cramped position, grinning blandly, and feeling rather like an " Aunt Sally."

The specialities of every confectioner in Halminster were done ample justice to by all except Fräulein, who laughed and talked too much to eat. But she tasted everything, and said it was all excellent. Her eyes glistened with enjoyment, and George was well repaid for his trouble. The close quarters made them all the merrier. It wouldn't have been half the fun if they had had plenty of room to move their legs in, and hadn't been obliged to put their plates in their laps ; or if, when George got up to propose Fräulein's health, he hadn't bumped his head against a bracket on which a beloved monstrosity in the shape of a brass elephant reigned supreme. The bracket, unused to such rough treatment, came toppling down, bringing with it a shower of peacocks' feathers, a photograph of the College Eleven, and a formidable-looking dagger. This little incident made the whole party shout with laughter, except George, who picked up his precious ornament with a somewhat rueful countenance, and just for a moment rather repented his hospitality.

It seemed as if the twins had mutually determined that nothing should be left of the good things, for, long after

every one else had had enough, they continued to " stodge,"
as Charlie expressed it.

"I wish the pater were here to tell us some of his
Indian adventures," said Hal. "We must have a story
from some one. Mike, you give us one."

Mike blushed and shook his head.

"I can't," he said. "But if only Aunt Nancy was
here! She is such a good story-teller."

"What a privileged being you are, Mikie! Nancy has
never favoured me with any of her stories," George said.

"Nor me either!" exclaimed Charlie and Hal simul-
taneously.

"Let Fräulein tell us a story," proposed Rosey; "I am
sure she can."

"Do! do!" was the general entreaty.

Fräulein's cheeks became as red as the ribbon she had
tied round her neck in honour of the party.

"The little black boy, dressed in that funny way,
reminds me of a story I read once, in one of our Gretchen's
books," she said in her simple manner, smiling at Jack.
"I will tell it if you really like, but it is not an adventure
or anything true. Perhaps you will think it silly."

"Is it a fairy story?" asked Rosey.

"It is not about fairies. We call it 'Märchen.'"

"Something after the style of the 'Arabian Nights,'
perhaps," George suggested. "Let us have it by all
means."

Thus encouraged, Fräulein began her tale, and very

prettily she told it.   Of course she used a great many odd words, but that only made it all the quainter and added to its charm.

If you would like to read the story, here it is—not exactly as Fräulein told it, because it wouldn't do to write down her funny expressions ; but as nearly as possible as it stands in Gretchen's story-book :—

CHAPTER XVIII.

FRÄULEIN'S MÄRCHEN.

THERE was once a poor little Blackamoor, who was coal-black, but not genuine for all that, because the colour came off. Every evening when he took off his clothes his shirt-collar was quite black, and when he caught hold of his mother's dress he left five finger marks on it. So she wouldn't let him come near her; if he did, she pushed him away and scouted him. Other people treated him even worse.

When he was fourteen years old his parents said it was high time he began to learn a trade by which he could earn his bread. Then he begged them to let him go out into the wide world and be a musician, for that was all he cared about.

But his father thought it was not a bread-winning art, and his mother got quite angry, and said, "Stuff and nonsense, you can't be anything but something black."

At last they came to the conclusion that he had better be a chimney-sweep. So they apprenticed him to a master, and because they were ashamed of his being a Blackamoor, they pretended they had made him black before he was apprenticed to see how it suited him.

Thus the little fellow became a sweep, and was forced

to creep up the chimneys from morning till night. They
were often so narrow that he was sometimes afraid he
would get stuck fast in them, but he always managed to
come out on the roof safe and sound, although he did feel
sometimes as if he had left his hair and skin behind.
When he sat high up on the top of the chimney, breathing
God's pure air once more, and the swallows flew round
him, he felt as if his heart must burst. He would shout
and sing for joy, and make the people in the street below
look up.

"Just look at the little black monkey up there!" they
would say. "What a voice he's got!"

As soon as he had learnt the trade, his master ordered
him to wash and make himself tidy. He said he was
going to discharge him now, for he was no longer an
apprentice but a journeyman.

The poor little Blackamoor trembled, and was seized
with a sickening anxiety. He said to himself, "It will
all come out now!" And so it happened. For when
he entered the master's room where all the apprentices
were assembled, he was still as black as ever, except for
a few light patches where the black had rubbed off in the
chimneys when he had grazed himself against the sides.
Every one gazed at him with horror. The master declared
he couldn't be a journeyman now, as he wasn't a decent
Christian. The pupils fell on him, dragged off his clothes,
and carried him into the yard. There they laid him under
the pump, and, in spite of his struggles, held him there

while they pumped on him and scrubbed him with straw and sand till he was sore all over. When they saw it was all of no use, and that hardly any of the black came off, they hooted and kicked him out into the street, and shut the back-door on him.

There he stood in the middle of the street, without clothes, not knowing what to do. It chanced that a man came by, who looked at him from head to foot, and when he saw that he was black, he said that he was a distinguished gentleman, and would take him into his service. He should have nothing to do but stand behind his carriage with folded arms, when he and his wife drove out, so that people might know what fine folk they were.

The little Blackamoor didn't think twice about it, but went with the gentleman, and at first all went well. The distinguished man's wife became fond of him, and every time she passed him stroked his cheek. He had never met with such attention as this in his whole life before. One day when they went for a drive a fearful thunderstorm came up quite suddenly, and the rain fell in torrents. When they reached home the gentleman noticed that black drops were trickling down the back of the yellow carriage. He roughly demanded of the little Blackamoor what the meaning of it was. He got dreadfully frightened, and because he couldn't think of anything better to say, answered, he supposed as the clouds were black it had rained black drops.

"Fiddlesticks!" replied the grandee. He took out his

fine cambric handkerchief and licked the corner, which he
drew across the little Blackamoor's brow The corner was
quite black.

"I thought as much," he cried. "You aren't one bit
genuine.   A pretty discovery!   Go and find another
place!   I can dispense with your services."

Then the poor little Blackamoor packed his bundle and
prepared to go.   But the wife of the distinguished man
called him to her, and said that it was a great pity her
husband had found it out.   *She* had known it for a long
time.   Of course it was a great misfortune to be born a
Blackamoor, especially one whose colour came off!   But
he mustn't be faint-hearted, but brave and good, and then
in time he would get the same colour as other people.
She bade him farewell, and gave him a fiddle and a mirror
in which he was to look at himself every week.

So the little Blackamoor went out into the world and
became a musician.   Of course he had no master to teach
him how to count, or to play a piece over to him.   His
music-lessons were the songs of the birds, the rustling of
the trees, and the tinkling of the brooks, which he
listened to and tried to imitate.   Afterwards he got to
know that the flowers in the wood, and the stars in the
dark midnight sky, made their own especial music, which
even when it is quite still not every one hears.   This was
more difficult to imitate.   The most difficult thing of all
was to play like the beating of men's hearts.   He wandered
far and wide, and lived through much before he learnt that.

Sometimes it fared well with him on his wanderings, but oftener badly. If he stopped in the evening before some house, played a tune and begged shelter for the night, they would let him in. But when they saw the next morning how black he was and how his colour came off, they wouldn't have anything more to say to him, and abused and cuffed him till he went away. He didn't lose heart though, but thought of what the wife of the fine gentleman had said to him, and went fiddling on from town to town, and from country to country. Every Sunday he looked at himself in the mirror to see how much black had rubbed off. Certainly it wasn't much from one Sunday to another, but still it was something, and when he had wandered five years the white at the bottom began to glimmer through. Meanwhile he had become such a master of his instrument that wherever he came, young and old flocked to hear him.

One day he found himself in quite an unknown town, where reigned a Gold Princess. She had hair of gold and a face of gold, and hands and feet of gold. She ate with a golden knife and fork from a golden plate, drank golden wine, and had on golden clothes. In short, everything on her and round her was gold. For the rest she was intolerably proud and haughty, and although her subjects earnestly wished her to choose a prince and marry him she wouldn't do it because there was not one beautiful and noble enough for her.

Every day six princes were brought to her as suitors,

who had arrived in the town the night before. Then, far and wide, the one subject of conversation was the Gold Princess and her beauty.

The six princes were obliged to stand in a row before her throne, and she searchingly examined every part of them. At last she turned up her nose and said—

"Chase all six of them out of the town this minute. I can't bear the sight of them."

Immediately twelve gigantic attendants appeared with birch-rods the length of a man, and drove the whole company out of the town. So it went on every day, year after year.

When the little Blackamoor heard how beautiful the Princess was, he couldn't think of anything else. He went to her palace, sat on the marble steps, took his fiddle in his hand, and played his choicest airs.

"Perhaps she will look out of her window," he thought, "then I shall get a glimpse of her."

He had not played long before the Gold Princess commanded her waiting-maids to see who was playing so beautifully outside.

They brought her news that it was a man with the most extraordinary complexion they had ever seen. One declared it was mouse gray, another that it was drab as a mushroom, a third that it was brown as coffee.

Whereupon the Princess said they must bring him in so that she might judge for herself what colour he was.

The waiting-maids went down and brought him to

their mistress, and when he beheld the Princess, who really was gold from top to toe, and shone like the sun, he was at first so dazzled he was forced to shut his eyes. But when he could screw up enough courage to look at her properly, he felt as if he could not help himself, and threw himself on his knees before her, crying,

"Most lovely Gold Princess! You are more beautiful than you have any idea of; I am a poor little Blackamoor, who gets whiter every day; and that air I played is not by a long way the prettiest I know. You certainly must have a husband; and if you will marry me, I shall jump out of my skin almost with delight."

As the Princess listended to this, she first made a face like a duck's in a thunder-storm, for she was not over clever, in spite of all her beauty, and then she laughed till she was obliged to hold her sides, and the waiting maids laughed with her, then all of a sudden the twelve giants with the birch rods appeared, and when they saw who knelt before tho Princess, they set up a laugh that echoed through the whole town.

It now occurred to the little Blackamoor that he had said something foolish. With a great fear in his heart he seized his fiddle, tore open the door, and sprang down the stairs three steps at a time. Then he ran through the town across country to the nearest wood. There he threw himself on the grass, dead tired, and cried till he might have swam in his tears.

At last he was calmer, and said to himself, "When the

coachman is drunk the horses bolt! Are you clever, or are you stupid? You wished to marry the Gold Princess, therefore you are utterly stupid. You needn't be surprised if people laugh at you."

Thereupon he slung his fiddle over his shoulder, and wandered on, as before, from town to town, and from country to country. And year after year he became whiter and whiter, and won more and more hearts, for the melodies he composed were more exquisitely beautiful than ever, and he hadn't his match on the fiddle. And as he grew to manhood, he looked quite as white, nay, almost whiter than most other people. Nobody would believe he had ever been a Blackamoor.

It happened that he came once to a spot where an annual fair was going on. Here he saw a booth with a red curtain before it, which might have been new long ago, but was now ragged and full of patches. Near it, stood a dirty fellow in a gay coat, who blew a trumpet, and shouted to the people to walk in and see the greatest wonders of the world; a calf with two heads, a pig that could handle the cards and tell your fortune, and the world-famed Gold Princess, whom all princes had gone mad about.

"Can it be your Gold Princess," said he, and he went in.

He felt as if he could sink into the earth with horror, for it was really she. But the gold was peeling of in a hundred places, and he could see she was only made of tin.

" Goodness gracious ! " he exclaimed, " how did you come here, and what don't you look like ? "

" What's the matter ? " she replied, as if there was nothing to be surprised at. However, after she had looked at him long and closely, and felt sure she had seen him before, when she was still gold all over, she added wrathfully, " Do you imagine that people keep the same for ever, you silly duffer ? Your own nose has grown much longer."

At this he nearly laughed out loud, for he saw she did not recognise him. Yet he thought he would like to let her know who he was, so he asked her if she didn't remember him. He was the little Blackamoor whom she had long ago so cruelly laughed to scorn.

Now she began to look ashamed of herself, and with great choking sobs related how—first in only two or three places, then everywhere—the gold had begun to come off; how she had hidden it from her subjects, till they had at last noticed it and hunted her away. Now she was carried about from fair to fair, but she had had enough of it, and, if he were still willing, she would marry him.

He answered her very gravely that he pitied her from the bottom of his heart, but he had more sense than to marry a Tin Princess. He certainly hoped one day to find a better wife than that. He went out of the booth and left the Tin Princess almost bursting with rage.

" Nigger, wretched nigger boy, black as coal ! " she screamed after him. Nobody knew whom she meant, because there was no longer an atom of black left on his body.

He went his way soberly, and was glad that he never chanced to meet that dreadful person again. For some little time he continued his wandering life, then, when he had seen nearly the whole world, and began to be tired of roaming, it happened that the king heard of his wonderful playing and summoned him to his Court. He played to him till long after midnight, and the king was so enchanted that he stepped down from his throne, embraced him, and asked him if he would be his bosom friend. He readily consented, and the king let him drive through the town in his golden coach, gave him a house, and so much money that it was enough to last him all his life. And he had a wife too. Not a princess, it is true, nor gold from top to toe, but a wife with a golden heart. He lived with her happy and content till the end of his days.

The Tin Princess became day after day more unpresentable, and when the last bit of gold peeled off, she was tossed hither and thither, and treated as a mere deformity and encumbrance.

At last she was lodged at a pawnbroker's. There she stands in a corner till this day, with a lot of musty old frippery and rubbish, and has time to consider that many things pretty, as well as ugly, wear out in this life, and therefore it matters a great deal what is underneath. *(From the German of Leander.)*

CHAPTER XIX.

"OH, MOTHER, MOTHER!"

MIKE went back to Mr. Parkinson's after Easter, and worked with almost feverish zeal. Those lightly spoken words of his father's "I shall expect to find you quite a scholar when I come back," continually rang in his ears, and fired him with ambition. Yet Mike wasn't a book-worm. He often joined in his school-fellows' games, and had many a grand wrestle with Carrots, who, though he generally got the worst of it, bore no malice, and sometimes asked him to tea on half-holidays. His mother, a kindly, buxom woman, said he was the prettiest, best mannered boy she had ever seen, and exhorted Carrots to open the door for her as Mike did when she went out of the room, and to show other polite little attentions which she had never believed boys capable of, till she had known Mike.

"That kind of thing wouldn't go down, if I tried it, mother. I am not made of the same stuff as Fitzgerald."

"No, Dick, you aren't indeed," sighed Mrs. Carrots. Dick had not introduced red hair into his family, but inherited it. "His poor young mother, how proud she must have been of him."

"He's got plenty of people to be proud of him still,"

Carrots rejoined. "The Hayworths think an awful lot of him."

"Ah! all the aunts and uncles in the world don't make up for a mother. You'd find that out, Dick, if I died, and you went to your aunt's."

"My aunts are such old girls though. Now the Miss Hayworths are regular clinkers."

Then seeing tears in his mother's eyes, he gave her a rough embrace, and said, "You aren't going to die yet, old mother. What would become of me without you, I should like to know?"

And Mrs. Carrots thought as she had thought a hundred times before, that she wouldn't change her boy for any other in the world, or have one hair on his fiery head different from what it was, although he did rub velveteen knickerbockers white in no time, tear rents in his stockings that baffled the art of darning, and cost her a small fortune in shoe-leather.

Aunts and uncles don't make up for a mother, that was true indeed. Much as Mike had got to love his, he would have given them all up, even devoted Nancy, to have back just one day of the old life—a day of the sweet companionship of her, whom God had taken to himself in the fair bright morning of her life, sparing her perhaps a grey toilsome noon, and a night of weariness and sadness. Her white robed figure, standing with arms outstretched to receive him, and to draw him down on some cool green bank, and perhaps hear all he had to tell of the great struggle below, was the boy's picture of heaven. He saw it all as he lay on his little iron bedstead, after Nancy had gone, for she still kept up coming to say "Good night," and to have a little chat with him before going to bed.

"Perhaps I shall be a man," he thought once, "and she won't know me when I come. Oh, if she took some other little fellow in her arms instead of me, and let me stand by unnoticed, how could I stand it. But God won't let that happen, for it wouldn't be heaven if she didn't know me."

One night when George was in the throes of a geography paper which had been allotted to the victims of the last Army Examination, he fancied he heard a low sobbing moan in the room above him.

"Surely Mike is asleep. He can't be crying. It must be the wind," he said to himself.

However, he felt he must go upstairs to make sure. The house was quiet, as the younger members of the family were gone to bed, and the elder ones had not yet left the drawing-room. The door was ajar, and George heard a poor little stifled voice murmuring—

"Oh, mother, mother, if I could only come now! Must I wait till I am a man! So long! so long! I know I am not good enough to come. Mother darling, if God would just let you come back to me for one minute to tell me how to be good, how to forgive *him*, it would be so much easier."

Then there was another piteous sob, and George went back to his study with a choking sensation in his throat.

An hour later, when Mrs. Hayworth went to look at her grandson, as she often did at night, she found him asleep with his head buried in the pillow.

"Funny boy to lie like that," she whispered softly, bending down to kiss one of the firm brown hands that lay outside the clothes.

She little guessed what a tear-stained, sorrow-stricken face lay hidden there. A face that wore a much older and more careworn expression than her own. Time dealt kindly with Mrs. Hayworth; her brow was smooth, her cheeks still round and pink, and everyone who saw her with her stalwart boys and tall daughters round her, marvelled at the youthfulness of her appearance.

George looked anxiously at his nephew next morning, expecting to see a heavy-eyed, pale, little Mike, and was pleasantly surprised to discover no traces of last night's grief on his handsome face. If anything, he was less grave than usual, and laughed quite heartily at the General's jokes.

"He mopes when he is by himself, that's what it is," thought George. "He oughtn't to sleep alone."

But he did not make any suggestion that the sleeping arrangements should be changed, as at first he had thought of doing, for somehow or other he could not bring himself to mention Mike's sorrow to his mother or the girls. It seemed too sacred a subject to discuss. *They* took it for granted that Mike was at last reconciled to his motherless lot, and "beginning to forget," as all children do in time.

At the end of the summer term, Mr. Parkinson invited the parents and friends of his boys to witness the distribution of prizes. Everyone was pretty confident that Mike would carry off one at least, although he shook his head when such a possibility was hinted at.

"It is a great pity," said Flo, looking at the date on Mr. Parkinson's card, "but I think hardly any of us will be able to go."

"Why not?" exclaimed Nancy.

"Because, to begin with, mamma is going to the Livingstones' at Crabstow, and Maud and I certainly must go with her," answered Flo, who was a great adept at remembering engagements and seeing that they were kept. "Then papa and George will not be back from London, and you and Rosey are going to your picnic with the High School girls."

"Bother the picnic! Mike is sure to get a prize, and I wouldn't miss seeing him go up for it for anything."

"But Nancy," objected Rosey, "you can't possibly give up going to the picnic, especially when you are one of the committee."

The High School girls, being far too vast a body to go anywhere together, each form had its picnic separately. The choice of provisions was vested in a committee of three, who had a meeting to discuss what viands would be the most practicable to take to a picnic, and then when they had settled, undertook to purchase them.

Nancy had entered into the whole affair with much zest, but now was all eagerness to give it up. Mike would feel so desolate, she thought, going up for his prize with no one there to care, while all the other little Parkites would have their mothers and sisters beaming on them.

"Fräulein shall go instead of me. She would like to see Brinley Abbey!" Nancy said, going up to Fräulein, who stood knitting in the school-room window, and twining her arm round her waist. For Nancy had "come round" at last, as George said, and was doing her best to make up for her former cold, ungracious conduct towards the poor little home-sick German, who, now that they were all kind to her, was as lively and happy as possible.

"You know well enough, Nancy, that no one may come who doesn't belong to the High School," said Rosey impatiently.

"Flo," appealing to her elder sister, "Nancy must come to the picnic, mustn't she?"

Flo shrugged her pretty shoulders.

"My dear Rose," she said, arranging some flowers on the mantel-piece, "you talk as if I had the control of Nancy's actions, instead of its being so very much the reverse."

"Well," said Nancy, good-humouredly, "I should be very glad if you would control them next Thursday after-noon, at half-past three o'clock, in the direction of Mr

Parkinson's. Really, Flo, I wish you would ask mamma
to let me off the picnic."

"I am sure mamma won't force you to go if you really
prefer being stuffed up in a hot room with a crowd of
little boys, to driving in a break and four horses with all
your school friends. Brinley Abbey is such a lovely place,
too. I wish I was going. Look, Fräulein, how gay I
have made the vases!"

Fräulein had a great capacity for admiring, and poured
out lavish praise on Florence's skill in arranging flowers.

Nancy was rather vexed at the conversation being
changed so abruptly, and she went to see what her mother
had to say on the subject.

"If the weather is as uncertain as it is to-day, I shall
not object at all to your abandoning the picnic," Mrs.
Hayworth said. "You have such a heavy cold in your
head, and getting your feet wet in that long grass might
send it to your chest. But if it is a fine, hot day, it is a
pity you should miss the chance of going into the country.
Fräulein and Kathy might go and see Mike get his prize."

"Kathy!" exclaimed Nancy, contemptuously. "She's
nobody. I mean she would go to sleep," she added,
quickly.

CHAPTER XX.

WHEN the day came it was fine, and if not hot, breezy and sunshiny. But Nancy, as she walked back from school at half-past twelve, discovered a good sized black cloud behind a company of shining white ones. "Now if that would only burst, mother would call the weather unsettled, and I should be all right," Nancy said to herself.

At a quarter to two Rosey was ready to start, and calling for Nancy at the bottom of the stairs to make haste.

"Oh dear, why doesn't she come!" she exclaimed, stamping her little foot impatiently. "We had to be at the top of High Street at ten minutes to two. Just like Nancy to keep everybody waiting."

"Go and hurry her up," said Hal, who was playing catches with Charlie in the hall. The heavy cricket ball clicked into his hand, and then out again as he spoke, rolling along the floor into the umbrella stand, and causing Charlie to howl "Butter-fingers," at the pitch of his voice.

Rosey found Nancy deliberately drawing on her gloves, a thing she as a rule never did till she was outside the house.

146

"Well, Nancy, you *are* dawdling. I have been ready for at least ten minutes. What have you put on your ulster for?"

"Because there is a huge black cloud coming up as fast as it can," said Nancy, with a very weather-wise air. "That white frock of yours looks very nice *now*, but you wait, you'll look like a drowned rat before long."

"Nonsense! That cloud is sure to pass over, I think, and if it doesn't, we shall only have a shower. I promised Fatima I would wear white, because she wanted me to be like her. Now do come, Nancy."

Nancy felt her cloud was deserting her in the hour of need, and followed Rosey, who was very festively attired, in a pretty white dress, with a broad black sash, and a large straw hat. She peeped into Mike's little room on her way downstairs. He was putting on a clean collar, and brushing himself up for the prize giving.

"It's not going to rain after all, Mike, so I must go to the picnic, or mamma will be vexed."

'Of course, I hope you will enjoy yourself very much, Aunt Nancy."

"But it's a shame that you should have no one to clap you."

"Oh, the fellows will clap enough, if there is anything to clap me for! Good-bye, Nan. I hope you will have a jolly time," and he turned round from the looking-glass and gave her a kiss, which she would like to have returned with fifty; but she knew he didn't care for too much demonstration.

"It would have been so jolly, Mike, to hear old Parky praise you, and the boys cheering. Oh, I forgot to get you a button-hole! What a pity. Rosey is mad to be off, so I must go," and away she flew.

Just as they turned into the High Street, a few large drops fell on the pavement.

"It's beginning to pour!" exclaimed Nancy, rapturously, "Mamma said I was not to go if it was showery, because of my cold."

It was useless for Rosey to remonstrate, and to declare the rain was only sun-drops, for Nancy had turned tail, and was speeding back to Abercrombie square. She never stopped till she reached Mr. Parkinson's. When she had rung the bell she remembered she was an hour and a-half too early, and perceived that the rain had ceased altogether. She was too hot and breathless to say anything to the grinning "buttons" who opened the door. He showed her into the long school-room, where rows of chairs had been arranged in front of a raised platform, for the expected visitors, and forms at the back for the boys.

Mr. Parkinson, his five boarders, and two assistant masters, were only just finishing dinner.

"Who can that be?" said the schoolmaster, getting up from his cheese. "It surely isn't a boy come to the front door. I must go and see."

"Miss Nancy, how do you do? You are in good time."

Mr. Parkinson smiled down on her with a twinkle in his jolly brown eyes. She was a favourite of his.

"Yes, I made a mistake. Shall I go away again? I am afraid I shall be in the way."

"Not at all. There will be a swarm of boys in here directly, so come and wait in my study till some other ladies come. It will be more comfortable for you."

Then he began to ask her about George's examination, Rajah's jumping, and the last cricket match at the college, till she was quite at her ease, and not at all sorry she came so long before the time.

Before three all the boys were in the school-room, scuffling and chattering as only small boys can. Then some fathers and mothers arrived, and Nancy went and sat near them in the front row, to Mike's intense surprise, who naturally thought she was at the picnic.

Mrs. Carrots was there, looking very grand in a dark green satin, with a cream lace *fichu*, the point of which was very far from being in the middle of her broad back, and her fat hands so closely imprisoned in yellow kid gloves that she couldn't have clapped them, even if her son had been called up for a prize—a thing that had never happened yet, although he had been at the school since he was a mite of six.

Nancy's heart swelled with pride when Mr. Parkinson, after reading out the names of the boys in Mike's class, as they stood in the examinations, requested Fitzgerald to come up for the prize. Amidst vociferous cheering he walked up the long room, and stood with modestly downcast eyes while Canon Brown handed him a handsomely

bound copy of " Westward Ho ! " with a few words of
commendation.   It was not the only prize he got; two
more were awarded him—one for conduct and the other
for geography.   Each time he turned to walk back to his
place, he met Nancy's happy loving eyes, and thought it
was nice to have her there.   To see her so pleased was
better than all the applause of his school-fellows.

" What a small boy to do so much," said a lady, looking
at him through her double eye-glass.   " He is not so big
as my Ralph, and he is only in the third class.   He must
be very small for his age.   Who is he, I wonder ? "

" He is my nephew," said Nancy, proudly, " and he is
not at all little for his age."

The lady smiled at Nancy's eager glowing face, and
whispered to her husband—

" Isn't that excited child one of General Hayworth's
daughters ? "

" Ah, so it is," he answered.   " Very like the one that
married."

" Oh, no ! " and Nancy was subjected to an inspection
through the glasses, to her infinite disgust.   " Not *nearly*
as pretty ! " was the verdict spoken, loud enough for her
to hear.

The prizes were shown all round that evening by
Nancy, and cook and Jack were among the most enthu-
siastic admirers of them.   Charlie and Hal congratulated
Mike warmly, and said it was a pity the General wasn't
at home to tip him.

"The mater can do it for him," suggested Billy.

"Happy thought, William," said Charlie. "When you get your prizes we shan't have room for them all in the house, I expect. Jack had better bring down the wheelbarrow to the college to cart them home in!"

Billy took this chaff very stolidly, and was soon to be seen head downwards in the old arm-chair.

When Rosey came home from the picnic she looked rather like a "drowned rat," as Nancy had predicted. She said it had rained nearly all the time at Brinley. The eatables had got very moist. Fatima hadn't worn white, after all, but blue serge. Miss Vane, the governess in charge, had not allowed them to swing, and altogether Rosey was rather "put out."

"Do leave my things alone, Charlie!" she cried, fractiously, as that unmitigated tease put on her coal-scuttle hat, tied it under his chin, and holding up an imaginary dress, minced round the room on the tips of his toes.

"Sweet Fatty Headland to a T!" laughed Hal.

Rosey, exasperated at her friend's romantic name being thus vulgarly abbreviated, flounced out of the room. She was surprised that Nancy followed her instead of staying behind to laugh at the joke going on at her expense.

"You look awfully tired, Rose," she said kindly "shall I go and coax Hester to come and help you to undress?"

"Thank you, I *am* tired," said poor draggled Rosey, and then she began to think that Nancy had been much nicer lately than she used to be. There *was* a change in Nancy. She was less careless of people's feelings, not so rebellious against her elder sister's ideas of propriety, more gentle in her manners, and not nearly so tomboyish. Maud and Florence were obliged to admit that she was at last becoming a little more lady-like. What hard struggles Nancy had had with herself to accomplish that "little more *lady-likeness*" nobody knew, except Mike, her beloved little friend and helper.

CHAPTER XXI.

GRANDMAMMA FITZGERALD.

IT was the first week in August and every one's holidays had begun. The Hayworths spent most of their time in the Square, playing tennis or reading under the large chestnut tree. One baking afternoon the General came to the railings, holding his great white umbrella lined with green over him, and called Mike to come to him.

"There is a letter for you, my boy," he said. "You will find it on the dining-room chimney-piece."

"From father, perhaps;" and Mike's cheeks glowed.

He bounded away before the General could undeceive him, for he knew the letter was not from his father.

"Come and have a game of tennis, papa," shouted Nancy. "I should like to see you and Fräulein have a set single-handed."

Fräulein was being initiated into the essentially English pastime, and found even the scoring an unconquerable difficulty, although the boys declared she would be a first-rate player in time.

"No thank you, Nancy. Lawn tennis isn't the game for a gouty old wreck like me. Make that lazy fellow, George, play;" and the old Indian strolled on clubward.

George who has since his examination thought he was

at liberty to take things easy, was lying full length on a rug, with Rajah at his side and one of Whyte Melville's novels open before him. Every now and then he would start up on his long legs, tear his fair hair, and look like a madman.

"What is the matter?" the whole party would exclaim at once.

George groaned that he had just thought of some "awful blunder" he had made in one of his papers, and that he was "safe to be ploughed."

"Well, it's only your first shot, old Geordy, so you needn't mind much," comforted Hal.

"Rather a waste of brain, though," said Charlie, "for he'll have the trouble of laying in another stock of knowledge, as of course there is none of the last left."

Charlie got his ears pulled for "cheek," and then George resumed his languid posture and the thread of "Holmby House."

Mike's letter was from his Grandmamma Fitzgerald, and its contents were so pleasant that he forgot the momentary disappointment he had felt when he found his father had not written to him after all. The old lady wrote a beautifully clear hand, and Mike had no trouble in reading it. She had taken an old place called Cleve Court, near Cragford on the Moors, for two months, and she invited Mike to come and stay with her there. He was to bring as many of his aunts and uncles as he liked, and friends too if he had any, as the house was large

enough for a regiment. Mrs. Hayworth was to pack them
off as soon as convenient. She knew how to make young
people happy, so they had better come. The more the
merrier.

"Bring the dog you wrote so much about in your last
nice little letter. I can't bear to think of the poor beast
being shut up in the town all this beautiful weather;
there are two empty kennels in the yard."

"Rajah, too. Oh, this is splendid !" and Mike ran out
to the others, waving the letter above his head, and
shouting, "a jolly piece of news ! Auntie Nancy, just
read this out loud." Nancy obeyed. "Well, she is a
trump !" cried Charlie, when she had finished. "Will
you take me, Mike ?"

"Of course," said Mike, "all of you—Fräulein too ! "

"I can hardly realize it. It seems almost too jolly to
be true ! " Nancy said. "I am glad mother hasn't taken
those stuffy lodgings at Brinemouth."

"The grown-ups won't come, of course," said Hal.
"They would spoil it all." George told him he was not
to decide who should go, and who shouldn't, and as the
discussion began to get rather warm, Mike proposed they
should go in and consult Mrs. Hayworth.

Not many days afterwards, Nancy and Mike, Charlie
and Hal, Fräulein and the twins, Rajah and Jack, all
started for Cragford. It had only been decided at the
last that Jack should go. He had been ailing lately,
missing his open air life in the hot summer days, and

Nancy declared he wanted change as much as she did, and wrote to Mrs. Fitzgerald, in spite of all remonstrances to ask her if he might come, saying he would make himself very useful, and clean all their boots. The old lady gladly consented, so Jack came and acted quite the part of a little footman on the journey, looking after the luggage, and panting under a load of umbrellas, macintoshes, and tennis-racquets. From Milton to Cragford there was no railway, and to the intense delight of our party they had a ride on the top of a coach-and-four. Rajah was put inside with Jack to see that he behaved properly. The scent of the pure bracing air roused the dog in Rajah.

He rested his massive fore paws on the sash of the coach-window, and looked out with a low suppressed howl of longing, and an impatient swaying of his tail.

"Oh for a race over those purple hills," his wistful, red-brown eyes said as plainly as possible. How eloquent are dogs' eyes. More so, often, that the tongue of man. Every inch on the outside of the coach was crowded either with luggage or people, and the conductor said peremptorily, "No more room outside, sir," to a tall, thin clergyman, with a very pale face, who stood with his portmanteau in his hand, and one foot on the step as if he intended climbing up; he turned away with a weary disappointed air, and was about to resign himself to the inside, when Hal said, "We can make room for him here, Mike, you sit on my knee. Conductor, tell that gentleman there is room now."

"Thank you, very much," said the clergyman, as he wedged his spare form into the place between Hal and Nancy. "I haven't been in the country for such a long time, and I don't want to lose a breath of this invigorating air."

"Isn't it glorious!" said Nancy. "We live in the town, too; it's so stuffy and horrid."

He turned his sunken but beautiful eyes on the fresh, intelligent face beside him, to which the crisp moorland breeze had already brought a soft rich colour.

"What town is it you live in?" he questioned.

"Halminster—such a stuffy old place," answered Nancy, thinking with scorn of the narrow limits of the turf in the square as her eye wandered over the sweeps of beautiful undulating country which stretched on either side of the road they were briskly driving along.

"A pleasant city. You are fortunate to live under the shadow of a cathedral," he said, and sighed heavily. He was thinking of the dens and closely packed hovels of his parish in the East End of London, where scores of maidens the age of this one, fought for existence, and did not complain of "stuffiness" or an atmosphere reeking with bad smells, because they had been born and bred in it, and knew no other. Alas! for those who were dying in it without ever having drawn in one draught of God's pure air—without ever having seen one glimpse of the fair green world!

The coach stopped at the Blue Dragon in the quaint

old High Street of Cragford. Here there was a cart
waiting to take the Hayworths' luggage to Cleve Court,
which was a mile further on.

Jack went with it and Kathy, too, who declared she
was tired, but really was only lazy. The others were
delighted to walk through the fragrant lanes, where grew
long glossy ferns curling their spiral tips out of the way
of the foamy springs that gushed merrily down the high
hedges at intervals into a clear blue stream by the roadside.

They went through a white iron gate into a long shady
avenue of stately elms. A young woman with a baby in
her arms came to the door of the pretty little lodge, which
was covered with roses and clematis, and gave them a
smiling greeting.

"Master Mike," she said, "you remember me, don't ye?"

"Becky!" exclaimed Mike, recognizing one of Mrs.
Bumpkin's daughters. Her rosy beaming face reminded
him of those sad, dark days he had spent with Janet just
a year ago at the Cragford farm-house. He saw again
Becky wiping her hands after feeding the poultry to take
that letter from the postman which brought the news of
his precious mother's death, and then smuggled under her
apron for fear he should see it, because it had a black edge.

"You've growed wonderful, Master Mike," Becky went
on, not noticing the cloud on the young face, nor the
tears that gathered in the deep blue eyes. "And Janet
is married. You must tell her when you write to her
that I'm married too, and come to be lodge-keeper at

Cleve Court. Squire Vine was glad to get such a tenant as your gran'ma, and he'd like to see you young ladies and gentlemen enjoying of yourselves at the old place, I know."

When Fräulein had done admiring the tiny scarlet baby, which no one else could conscientiously bring themselves to do, they all went on to the house, Mike choking back his tears, for he did not want to damp the others' pleasure, and was glad that none of them but Nancy had seen he was crying. She gave his hand a sympathetic squeeze. *She* knew so exactly how he felt.

Mrs. Fitzgerald was standing to welcome them in the old portico. She was *quite* the orthodox grandmamma, with her silvery hair and fine lace cap, and softest of white woollen shawls pinned over her black satin dress.

"Welcome to the country, you dear town rats," she said, holding out her hands to them with a smile that won the boys' hearts. "This is my grandson, I know, though I haven't seen him since he was two. He looks graver than ever, I do believe. Now, introduce me. Which aunt is this? Nancy? I thought so. Aunt Katharine came with the boxes, and we are fast friends already. She is upstairs now, fixing where you shall all sleep, with Green, my maid. Oh, you beauty," patting Rajah, "you must be shown your bedroom too, mustn't you?"

So the old lady chatted on, and by the time they were all seated enjoying the spread she had prepared for them in the library, every one felt perfectly at home. Mike was told he was to act the part of host, and sat opposite his grandmother at the end of the long table. The twins' capacity for clearing dishes did not in the least alarm Mrs. Fitzgerald. She said they were the only two of them all who had what she considered a good healthy appetite. She shook her pretty old head at Fräulein, and told her in very good German that if she didn't improve and eat more to-morrow, she should send her home. "That boy's a book-worm," she said, nodding at Hal, who was greedily eyeing the books that lined the walls from floor to ceiling. "If he wants to mope over fusty old tomes all day he must go home too. I am only joking, my dear," she added; "you may feast on the books if you like. But they aren't mine, so you must take great care of them."

Hal would have begun directly after tea, only Charlie would not allow it, and made him go out with him to explore the garden. The others sat on the terrace, and watched the sunset, which made the queer stumpy old tower of Cragford church glitter against its background of dark green orchards and beechwoods. It was a beautiful view. On one side of them lay verdant fields and wooded slopes; on the other tiers of wild hills covered with bracken and regal foxgloves, and behind them rose a great dark shoulder of the heathery moor, with a rugged flank of gray rock, standing out sharply against the saffron sky.

"They tell me that is 'Greybeard's Tor,'" Mrs. Fitzgerald said. "You must all go for a picnic there one day. Perhaps Mr. Pelham, who has come to take the vicar's duty while he is in. Switzerland, will go with you, if he has the strength to climb hills, which I rather doubt, for I fear he has worked himself to a shadow among some of the London poor."

"He must be the gentleman who sat next me on the coach," Nancy exclaimed eagerly. "I never saw such a thin, pale face in my life! He had great holes in his cheeks, hadn't he, Mike?"

"Yes," said Mike. "But he had a nice kind voice, and looked very jolly."

"I don't know whether I liked him exactly. He seemed quite angry when I said Halminster was a stuffy place. I am sure it is. Fancy how unbearably hot it would be there this evening, while here it is quite cool."

"Chilly, I think, my dear. Come, we will go in. Shouldn't my grandson be going to bed, Fräulein?"

The old lady stepped lightly through one of the windows that opened on to the terrace as she spoke. She seemed to have all that makes old age beautiful, without any of its infirmities.

"I have set some of my own things about in this room," she said. "Here's my particular chair that I take with me wherever I go. There's no chair that I can rest in as I can in that one. And there are my pet photographs. This is a miniature of my Eddy when he was a boy. I wonder if any of you will think it like Mike."

She ordered the lamps to be brought that they might see it better.

11

" It's not a bit like our nephew," said Nancy, in her emphatic way, after a very short scrutiny.

" The shape of the head and the colour of the eyes are like," said Hal.   " But Mike's mouth is quite different, and his expression too."

Mrs. Fitzgerald took the miniature into her own hands again, and looked long and lovingly at the proud vindictive face of her handsome boy.

" Ah ! " she murmured, " it's like and it's not like. Mike got that thoughtful expression from his mother. Eddy was never very thoughtful.   But I thought him perfect and spoilt him.   He was my only one."

The cheerful old face suddenly looked sad and careworn, and the lovely Irish eyes, which contrasted so well with the snow-white hair, became misty.

Mike had not looked at the miniature at all, or heard what the others said about it.   He was intently gazing at a photograph of his mother dressed as Mary, Queen of Scots, which stood in a velvet frame on a small table at the other end of the room.

Nancy wondered what he was looking at, and came and stook by him, slipping her hand into his.

" Mother a queen," he whispered.   " Do you know, Aunt Nancy," he said, drawing her into a shadowy recess of the old-fashioned drawing-room, " I must have been very little, but I remember quite well seeing her dressed up like that.   Somehow I didn't like her dressed up, and *he* didn't either.   How pretty she must look in her angel's dress! Oh my darling angel mother, when shall I come to you?" He spread out his arms yearningly, and gazed wistfully before him. Nancy was frightened. "He's so good, perhaps he *will* go to her soon," was the thought that flashed across her for the first time, and filled her soul with horror.

"Mikie, don't, don't!" was all she could say as she threw her arms passionately round him, looking down on him with tears—rare visitors in her happy grey eyes, shining on her lashes. The lively group, sitting in the silvery lamp-light, asking riddles and showing each other card tricks, little suspected what was going on in the dark corner of the room. Nancy, who a few minutes before had been laughing with the rest, felt the depths of her warm young heart stirred till they seemed to come to the top, and only by squeezing and squeezing Mike, could she get them back to their proper place.

She wished that photograph had not been there, she was afraid Mike might go and stare at it, and get sad over it, much oftener than was good for him. At home all the pictures of their dear dead sister were locked away, so that Mike should not see them. But no one ever saw Mike look at the Queen photograph again. When he passed the little table where it was placed, which he was obliged to do every time he went in and out of the drawing-room, as it stood near the door, he turned his head resolutely the other way.

CHAPTER XXII.

THOSE were happy days at Cleve Court. The out-door life, the abundance of cream and home-made bread and butter "put new life into all of them," they said. As they were not very dead-alive before, they now brimmed over with spirits and fun. Grandmother, as Mrs. Fitzgerald made them all call her, said she felt younger for looking at the sunburnt, healthy faces, and hearing the youthful laughter and chatteration. Charlie and Hal had found that some schoolfellows of theirs were lodging at Mrs. Bumpkin's farmhouse, and went out with them every morning fishing, or butterfly hunting, and played cricket and tennis with them in the afternoon. The twins confined themselves almost altogether to the kitchen garden. Between its high sunny walls, covered with peaches, they would have been content to stay till Doomsday, Charlie declared. They said it was a good place for hide-and-seek. But Billy always hid behind a tall white raspberry tree, and Kathy in a strawberry bed, where she had discovered an aftermath of strawberries, and they generally forgot all about looking for each other. So it was funny hide-and-seek. Nancy, Mike, and Fräulein were agreed that to

164

climb up on the moor, and lie in the heather, was after all
the most delightful thing to be done. Rajah was quite of
the same mind. He didn't climb, but bounded up and
then down, over and over again, urging his companions on
with short, impatient barks. When they sat down he
would roll and burrow and sniff or tear round and round
in a circle, and then stop for a moment, trembling with
ecstasy. Fly, an old spaniel Mr. Vine had left behind
him, sometimes condescended to accompany the town-bred
puppy standing on the brink of dog-hood, and sat blinking
his bloodshot eyes cynically at his antics, as much as to say,
"Poor foolish young thing, when you get to my age you
won't think so much of a moor. But then I was always
a superior dog, and never forgot my dignity."

"There is such space up here, and one feels so near the
sky," Nancy said once, throwing herself down and pillow-
ing the back of her head on her crossed arms.

The soft cool breezes came sweeping over the gorse and
heather, straight from the misty line of sea that lay in the
far gray distance. They set the delicate heath bells ring-
ing, and Nancy heard their fairy music all round her, when
a portly bee in a seal-skin jacket and gold belt stopped its
loud humming.

"Life doesn't seem a battle here, only a delicious dream.
How pretty those clouds are. That long pearly feathery
one looks like an angel's wing shut outside heaven. Oh,
Fräulein, don't knit, do be idle for once!"

"I should not like to do nothing," said the industrious

little German. "Knitting is no trouble, I can do it and look round me too."

The gleam and click of the bright needles, as Fräulein swiftly plied them, reminded Nancy unpleasantly of a sock she had begun and promised her mother to finish while she was away as a kind of holiday task. It was not much more than begun, still, as several stitches were dropped, the picking up of which weighed heavily on Nancy's mind when she thought of the sock at all.

"Nancy, Mr. Pelham is coming up the side of the hill," Mike said, as he returned from a race with Rajah, panting and glowing.

"Hurrah! Let us go and meet him, Mike;" and she sprang to her feet, brushing the green spikes of the heather from her dress.

Mr. Pelham had become a frequent visitor at the Court, and Nancy was quite sure now that she liked him very much.

"We will help you up, Mr. Pelham," she cried, descending rapidly and surely the wild stony path the clergyman was labouring up. "Here give me the end of your stick, and I will pull in front. Mike, you push behind. Here we are!"

"Thanks to these energetic young people. I am up at last, Fräulein," he said, sitting down beside her on the purple carpet. "How beautiful it is. This air makes one feel a different creature."

Nancy thought he looked quite the same creature and

not a whit less pale and worn than the first time she saw him.

"Are you really better," she asked, wonderingly.

"Yes," he answered, dreamily. "I am as well as I ever shall be again here." They knew what he meant and were silent.

"Mr. Pelham, our brother George is coming down here for two or three days, and we must do the picnic to Graybeard's Tor while he is here. He has passed his examination, and we ought to make a great deal of him."

"What examination?" Mr. Pelham asked.

"For the army. All our boys are going to be soldiers," Nancy said, proudly.

"This little man, too?" Mike shook his head, and the colour deepened in his cheeks as Nancy answered,

"Oh, no. Mike is going to be a great traveller and explorer. He will write books about the countries he sees, like that book father was reading the other day. What was it called? 'Captain Somebody's ride to Khiva,' won't you Mike?"

He was standing erect, with his well-knit, sturdy little frame sharply defined against the blue sky, the sunlight gilding his closely cropped head. "Yes," he replied, with a flash of enthusiasm in his blue eyes, "that's what I shall do, see the world and bring home treasures."

"I used to think I would go, too; but there is no place like England," Nancy said, thoughtfully. "I shall live in one of those pretty little cottages in Cragford, and be a proper old aunt, with a cap and mauve streamers, after all, and when Mike comes home from his voyages, I shall have brown holland put on my stair carpets, and be dreadfully afraid of his spoiling my furniture. He will think me an old fidget, and perhaps give up coming to see me, and then I shall break my heart and——"

"Oh, auntie Nancy!" interrupted Mike, "you are only joking. You won't ever be an old maid."

"I am never going to marry, so I don't see what else I can be, unless I turn gipsy. That's what I should like, to live out of doors all my life, and never go into a house again. But people oughtn't to do what they like, ought they Mr. Pelham?"

"It is wisest to try and like what we don't like," he said, smiling sadly. "Shall I tell you what my dreams were, when I was a boy?"

"Yes, do please," said Nancy.

"I wanted, like many another lad who lives by the sea, and reads books of adventure, to be a sailor. My brother Edgar, who was older than I, had the same longing. We were our mother's only children, and we knew we couldn't both go to sea. She desired most earnestly that one of us should go into the Church, like our father had done, who died a week after I was born. Edgar was much cleverer than I was, and I thought in my secret heart that he ought to be the clergyman. I knew my mother would part more readily with me than Edgar, whom she almost idolized. The subject was never mentioned between us, but each knew what the other felt. We lived in the Isle of Man, and many a wild night we spent on the shore in the midst of all the terrible excitement of a shipwreck, while our mother prayed and wept at home. When I was twelve, and Edgar thirteen, an uncle offered to place one of us on a training-ship, and then it had to be decided which of us was to go to sea. I saw the great craving in my brother's blue eyes, as he read the letter.

"'Mother, I am the eldest, and I must go. I shall never be any good on land,' he said, then he looked at me, and his face changed.

"We were all silent for some minutes. I can now hear Edgar's voice when at last he spoke, it was so hoarse and strange.

"'Write at once to uncle, mother, and say, "Willy is coming!"'

"He went out without another word. I watched him leaping lightly down to the cove that lay beneath our garden, and saw him get into the 'Mary Ann,' and pull out to sea. I was in a transport of joy. The life I had dreamed of and longed for lay before me now without any obstacles; then Edgar of his own free will had said I was to go.

"'Mother, you will have your Edgar always with you,' I cried. 'Aren't you glad? I shall be your sailor boy.' She said she wished both of us would stay with her, and give up the thought of going to sea. She told me, as she

had told us often before, how much noble work we might
do as servants of the Church; how we might be heroes
at home as well as at sea; and much besides, which fell,
I am afraid, on deaf ears. My rejoicing was soon changed
into mourning.   On that fair, still afternoon a sudden
squall sprang up; the wind blew from the north-west,
lashing the sea into fury.   It swept all the fishing-boats
that had gone out that day back on to the shore, with
such terrific force that most of them were utterly de-
stroyed, and the whole beach was strewn with their frag-
ments.   It was supposed that my brother had turned the
'Mary Ann' in the direction of our cove, hoping to reach
it before the squall began; but, before he could attain his
object, his light craft was dashed with ruthless violence
upon the rocks, and he—I found him dead and bleeding
on the cove !   My only brother, my Edgar, who a few
hours ago had given up the ardent desire of his short life
time for my sake.   I felt now how much more cut out for
a sailor he was than I, with his fair hair, and blue eyes,
and his lithe, strong limbs.   Oh, why, when he went down
to the cove, hadn't I run after him, and told him I would
stay at home, or at least have thanked him for his goodness to me, instead of sitting dumb in my selfish joy and
satisfaction !   But even my own misery and remorse was
forgotten when I thought of my mother.   I vowed, as I
flung myself on my brother's damp, cold body, that I
would never leave her.   Just then I felt as if I hated the
sea, my brother's murderer.   But when my grief grew

older the thirst for a sailor's life seized me once more;
only with God's help I conquered it."

"And your mother, does she live with you now?"
Mike asked.

He had been listening with breathless interest to Mr.
Pelham's story.

"She died soon after my ordination."

He rose and looked fixedly for a few minutes at the
faint vision of sea lying in the far west. Then he turned
and smiled down on Mike's earnest quivering face.

"You see, my boy, it is not always the best to do
what we plan for ourselves. I can only be thankful to
God that He didn't let me have my way. I rejoice to
think that I have been His messenger to many whose
lives are joyless. Thousands are here in this Christian
England who live and toil without a ray of hope in their
dark souls of anything better in store for them beyond
this world. Wretched as they are, dirty and miserable as
are their homes, none of us should shrink from giving
them our sympathy and loving help, for they are our
brothers and sisters, and the Father of all would have us
do something to brighten their dull sad existence."

Spratt on his straw bed, with his great hungry eyes,
came vividly before Mike.

"I won't be a traveller," he exclaimed. "I will be a
clergyman like you, Mr. Pelham, if only I am good enough.
I will build a great house in some beautiful place like
this, and go and visit the dirty cellars and take the boys

away with me to live there, and teach them to be happy."

"That would cost a great deal of money," Nancy remarked practically.

"Would it, Mr. Pelham?" asked Mike eagerly.

"Not more than is spent on useless extravagances and selfish pleasures by only too many. Yours is a grand scheme, my boy. May you have the means to carry it out one day."

Mr. Pelham went home with them and played chess with Mrs. Fitzgerald in the low old-fashioned drawing-room, after a high tea, at which he ate nothing, to the amazement and distress of the boys, who couldn't understand any one not being ravenous in Cragford.

When Mike said good-night to him, he whispered, "I expect my mamma has made friends with Edgar in heaven."

"God bless you," Mr. Pelham said.

CHAPTER XXIII.

A MOORLAND MIST.

"HERE we are at Graybeard's Tor, at last!" exclaimed Nancy, with a deep-drawn sigh of satisfaction. Boys in flannels, airily-clad maidens, hampers, and dogs, were all gathered together in the shadow of the grand old rock, that looked as if it had climbed up the moor itself, sat down to look at the view, and never moved again.

"I am sure I must be a pale shade of brown after that scorch, if not such a deep coffee colour as the rest of you," said George, fanning himself with his straw hat.

"Indeed you are not. You are as pasty as ever."

"You girls are jealous of my lily complexion. Nancy is as black as an ayah, or the little fiddler of Fräulein's story, and Kathy has freckles the size of counters all over her nose."

"Fräulein, do tell George not to make personal remarks, he minds what *you* say," said Nancy, mischievously. "We must have lunch now. Jack, undo the hamper."

"Hamper! You mean hampers," said Charlie. "I believe there's one each."

Charlie exaggerated, certainly, but there was indeed a goodly array of hampers. Mr. Pelham had brought one; and Mrs. Bumpkin had insisted on the Joneses, Charlie and

Hal's friends, who with their sisters were of the party, making their contribution to the picnic. Nancy wanted to have the cloth laid on the tor itself, which, she declared, would make a splendid table, but as the majority were strongly in favour of staying where they were in the shade, she was obliged to give in.

"If we had the stodge up there," said Charlie, "it would be a case of—"

"Thirteen picnickers, guzzling in the sun,
  All of them were frizzled up, and then there were none."

Mr. Pelham and Fräulein made an excellent salad between them, and Nancy and Lily Jones laid out the luncheon in a most approved style, with the aid, or as they said, *hindrance*, of the boys. There was a perfect regiment of cold ducks and chickens, all vieing with each other in plumpness. Rajah evidently thought that among so many one would not be missed, and was caught by Jack making off with the very fattest in his mouth.

Fly looked scandalized, and felt more contempt than ever for his juvenile companion.

"What presumption for that giddy creature to imagine he is entitled to a *whole* duck," he thought, "when *I* consider a drum-stick as much as I deserve."

After all there weren't too many provisions, for there was little left to take home, except empty pie-dishes, plates, and ginger-beer bottles.

It was decided that those who wanted to walk back to Cragford over the moor should start earlier than the rest, as it was a long way, and dangerous in the twilight. So at half-past six most of the party set off, leaving Mr. Pelham, who did not feel equal to the walk, with Mike, the twins, Lily Jones, and Jack. Nancy was rather unwilling to leave her nephew. The boys said he would be tired out if he came, but if Nancy stayed behind too they would never believe she was a good walker again.

"We can stay here another three-quarters of an hour," Mr. Pelham said. "Shall we walk about, or sit still and talk?"

"Sit still and talk," said Mike. "Tell us about London, Mr. Pelham."

"It's so cool now, we want to run races," said Kathy, who objected to the plan of doing nothing but talk. She thought Mr. Pelham a great deal too grave. "Jack, you must give us a start, as of course you are a splendid runner."

"Oh, no I ain't, Miss Kathy, not in boots," and Jack looked at his well-shod feet rather regretfully. Just for once he forgot to be proud of his respectability, and longed for a scamper barefoot over the heather. However, in spite of his boots, Jack managed to win all the races, and Billy confessed himself beaten hollow.

"Do you see that funny sort of grey cloud rising out of the ground?" asked Mike. "I have been watching it for five minutes, and it seems to get bigger and bigger."

Mr. Pelham looked in the direction Mike was pointing to, and saw a thin, cold wreath of mist creeping stealthily from the sea, and gradually encroaching on the clear blue hills.

"It comes from the sea, not from the ground," he said. "What an ugly blur it makes on the bright, fair landscape."

"We won't look that way. Let us go the other side of the tor," Lily Jones suggested.

They changed their places, and watched the great brown shadows trembling on the far-stretching expanse of moor, over which the others were walking with the dogs.

"They are out of sight at last," said Billy, as the distant figures disappeared altogether from their view. "I believe they will get home before us after all."

"Perhaps they will, if they keep up that pace. We had better be going down to the road to meet the waggon," Mr. Pelham said, looking at his watch.

The shawls and hampers were collected, and they were turning towards the precipitous path that led down from the tor, when they all sent forth an exclamation of dismay. A dense white mist drifted in their faces, and was rapidly enveloping every object to right and left of them.

"We must hurry down, and try to reach the road before it closes in all around us," Mr. Pelham said. "The girls had better keep near me."

But there were so many loose, sharp stones, and stunted bushes in their path, that it was impossible "to hurry down," and in a few minutes they could not see an inch before them. It was as if a great chilly veil had been clasped round them. Lily Jones was frightened, and began to cry. Billy remarked that it was worse than a London fog, and Kathy said she was wet to her eyelashes already.

"We had better sit down, for I fear we may fall if we go on. I hope the others are off the moor by this time."

"Oh, Mr. Pelham, shall we have to say here all night? Oh, how dreadful! We shall die of cold!" and Lily lamented loudly, and would not be comforted with Mr. Pelham's assurances that a sea mist departed generally as quickly as it came. Mike was silent. He had stumbled over a stone before Mr. Pelham bid them halt in their scramble down the hill, and had far more reason to cry than Miss Lily Jones, as he had given his ankle a nasty twist, and was in great pain. When they had sat for a long dreary half hour huddled up together, and wet to the skin, Mr. Pelham felt five firm fingers clasp over his. He could not see, but guessed they were Mike's.

"How are you getting on, little man?" he asked.

"Pretty well, thank you, Mr. Pelham," he answered in an alarmingly faint voice. "Wouldn't it be nice to sing 'Lead, kindly Light.' Jack, Aunt Nancy has taught you that hymn, hasn't she?"

"Yes, Master Mike, but I don't know the tune of it," answered Jack, rather shy at the idea of being called upon for a solo.

Mr. Pelham relieved him by beginning to pour forth in

12

his fine baritone voice the most poetical hymn in our language. Billy and Kathy joined in the second verse, but their feeble pipings ceased long before the end.

"Would you mind very much singing the last verse again?"

Mr. Pelham obeyed, and once more the beautiful words rolled out—

> "So long Thy power hath blest me, sure it still
>   Will lead me on,
> O'er moor and fen, o'er crag and torrent, till
>   The night is gone.
> And with the morn those angel faces smile,
> Which I have loved long since, and lost awhile."

"Thank you very much," said Mike.

"My boy, are you very wet and tired?" Mr. Pelham inquired affectionately, putting his arm round him.

"Yes, but it doesn't matter for me. I am afraid of your catching cold. It would be very sad if you went back to London ill. All the fresh strength you said you had got would be wasted. I can see your face quite plainly now, Mr. Pelham. Oh, look!"

A golden ray had pierced the mist, and they saw above them a patch of soft blue ether, flecked with dreamy, rosy cloudlets. Like magic the foggy cloak dropped gracefully from hills and moor, and gradually dissolved, and the whole fair scene lay smiling beneath the setting sun, as if nothing had happened.

CHAPTER XXIV.

A TRIAL OF PATIENCE.

MR. PELHAM stood wrapt in speechless admiration, but was soon roused to action by the fretful complaints of Lily Jones.

"Why didn't they go on now it was fine?" she asked.

"Jack," he said, "you run on to that cottage I see the other side of those fields, and herald the arrival of a wet party. The first thing to be done is to dry ourselves. I daresay we shall find the conveyance that Mrs. Bumpkin was going to send to meet us somewhere near at hand."

Mike made a noble effort to walk but fell with a suppressed groan after a few steps. "My foot hurts rather," he explained, and he lay white and faint on the drenched bracken. Mr. Pelham lifted him on his arms and carried him as gently as he could over the rough ground. He saw by the expression on the small face that every jerk was acutely painful to him. The twins trudged silently by his side, and Lily slid about some way behind, angry that no one took any notice of her whimperings. As she could no longer have any reason to think her life in danger, her frock was her grievance. A hundred times she wished aloud that she had put on a cotton dress instead of a French cashmere. Mr. Pelham at last silenced her by sharply telling her it was no good to cry over spilled milk, and till they reached the cottage she said no more about her unfortunate terra-cotta costume. Then she would not allow it to be set before the fire for fear it should cockle. The consequence was she put it on again damp, and if she didn't get a violent cold in her head afterwards, she certainly deserved it.

It was dark when Mr. Bumpkin's light waggon turned into Cleve Court by the back entrance. To Mr. Pelham's immense relief, Rajah and Fly were both in the yard barking a hearty welcome, so he knew the others were safely home. Before they were out of the waggon, a lithe figure came bounding round from the front of the house.

"Mike! Mike, my darling, are you all right!" There was a motherly, anxious ring in the young voice.

"Yes, auntie Nancy," Mike shouted back as cheerily as he could. But why didn't he spring out of the waggon as Billy and Kathy did?

"Mr. Pelham, don't carry me please," Mike whispered. "Let me try and walk, or she will think I am very bad."

"How slow you are, Mike. I want to get hold of you to be sure you are really there. I have been fidgeting about you so."

"He has twisted his ankle," Mr. Pelham said, "and most heroically he has born the pain. All the time we sat waiting for the mist to clear, none of us even knew he was hurt."

"My nephew is a hero, Mr. Pelham. Didn't you know that?" said Nancy. She stood in the ruddy warm light that streamed through the latticed kitchen window, making a path across the cobble-stones. He thought the brilliant face turned up to his, in which the child and woman were so strangely mingled, something more than beautiful. A vision of it as it looked then came before him often and often afterwards as he went from one dreary home to another in those regions of ugliness, poverty and vice where he saw so many sadly different faces from the one that haunted him, and where he had spent the freshest energies of his manhood in the service of Christ. There he laboured in spite of weak health till his death a few months later. No one wrote his life or extolled his virtues in the newspapers. Only the sick he had visited, the naked he had clothed, the erring souls he had saved mourned for him bitterly. In another world, perhaps, "Angel faces that he had loved long since and lost awhile," smiled upon him.

*   *   *   *   *   *

It was not till many days after they had bid Grand-mamma Fitzgerald farewell and gone back to Halminster, that Mike could put his foot to the ground. It was a severe trial of patience, but Nancy's Nephew came through it triumphant.

"Bodily pain is nothing like so bad as that other sort of pain," he said, when some one praised him for being so good about his ankle. Perhaps only Nancy knew how

much of "that other sort of pain," as he called it, he was
capable of bearing.   It was the way he bore it that made
her assert so confidently and proudly that Mike was a
hero.

CHAPTER XXV.

ANOTHER VIOLET.

"I HAVE been fortunate enough to gather another Violet as sweet and pretty as the first."

This was how Mr. Fitzgerald announced to his wife's family the fact that he was engaged to be married a second time.

They were all very hurt and sore about it.

The General threw the letter from him in disgust, and his eyes were wet as he repeated, "Another Violet. The fellow can have no heart." I shouldn't like to say how much tobacco he consumed that day to pacify his feelings.

"He might at least have waited a little longer! Only a year and two months, and he pretended to be heart-broken," said Maud bitterly.

"I always thought he would marry again, but not so soon," was Florence's remark when she heard the news.

The boys were highly indignant. George wrote from Sandhurst quite a long dissertation on second marriages, and Charlie and Hal said a great deal that they had better have left unsaid; but on Nancy the blow fell heaviest. In all probability her nephew would leave her, and at that dreadful prospect she felt as if her heart would break.

Mr. Fitzgerald had written to Mike saying he intended to bring his bride to Crabstow, which was and always would be his favourite seaside resort. He did not know how long he might stay there, but naturally till he went abroad again he would be "willing to relieve Mike's grandparents of the responsibility of taking charge of him."

Those words looked terribly stiff and cold, and Mike, as he read them, was obliged to fight hard, not to let the old enemy master him, that angry bitter feeling towards his father which he called his giant.

"Mike, you won't go, dear. He will let you stay with us I am sure if mamma writes and asks him. Say you will stay."

Mike shook his head. "I must go to him, Aunt Nancy," he said.

"Will you like to go, Mike? Will you be able to bear hearing him call some one else by *her* name?"

"Don't make it harder for me, Nancy," he sobbed. "It is my duty. You know what Mr. Pelham said about duty. I want to remember all he said. I want to be like him when I am a man, and to be some good."

"But think of me, Mike. What shall I do without you? How shall I get on with the battle all alone? I cannot talk to anyone as I can to you. Oh, you don't know what a lot I love you, or you wouldn't wish to leave me!" and Nancy buried her face in her hands in an agony of grief.

"Wish to leave you! Oh, Aunt Nancy," he exclaimed, reproachfully. "I thought you understood me better than that. Don't cry," he went on after a long pause, in which Nancy did not change her doleful position. "We shall see each other very often. Crabstow is so near."

"He hates us all. He never liked us to come even when she asked us," moaned Nancy. "It's no good, Mike; I can't bear it. If you go I shall be miserable."

"But when I am a man you shall come and keep house for me. Let us look forward to that," said Mike almost brightly. In his desire to comfort her he forgot the pain at his own brave heart.

CHAPTER XXVI.

"NOT YET."

SO Mike went back again to little Crabstow, and heard once more the familiar voice of the great blue sea. Nothing was changed. There were the patient donkeys standing on the beach, the great rough boys, and Mrs. Jenkins looking as fat and irritable as ever. Children built sand-forts like the one Nancy had engineered on that birthday of Mike's long ago, and the nurses and governesses sat with their work under the cliff. In the pretty garden of the old home the carnations bloomed as brightly as ever, but there was no sleepy old Roland lying on the lawn; no sweet mother watching at the window.

An old gentleman in a white waistcoat sat reading the "Times" in a garden-chair, quite oblivious of the pair of earnest dark blue eyes gazing at his domain.

Mr. Fitzgerald had taken a much larger house, which stood on the top of the cliff, in beautiful grounds. Instead of clumsy, silent James, there was a tall, grand footman, who glided noiselessly about, and looked at Mike, "the young shaver," as he called him in the kitchen, with lofty contempt. There were horses and carriages in the stables, and Mike wondered why his father had not had all these things when his own dear mother was alive. Did he think that *new* mamma deserved more? How could he think so? She was very handsome, but who could love her as well as her who, Mike was quite sure, had been the loveliest lady in the whole wide world.

His father did not take much notice of him. He had welcomed him kindly, and said he should have a private tutor till he was old enough to go to a public school. But days and weeks passed, and the tutor did not appear, and Mike felt dull and lonely, and longed for Nancy.

His beautiful stepmother bent her queenly head and kissed him every night and morning; that was the utmost of her motherly attentions.

"I wonder if she had a little boy who was really her own, whether she would play with him and talk with him as *she* used to with me? No, I don't think she would. She is too tall and her dresses are too grand for romping; and, as to talking, she doesn't talk much to father; only smiles at everything he says, and laughs sometimes that laugh which is always the same. She is just like a beautiful picture, except that she laughs and walks, and says 'Yes' and 'No.'"

This was how he mused, as he sat through the interminably long dinners at which he ate little or nothing.

The stately footman, with his deferential air, had something to do with his small appetite, he thought.

One sultry afternoon, after wandering aimlessly about the garden, he went into the drawing room. His father

and mother were gone out for a drive, so he threw him·
self languidly on a low comfortable chair in a corner of
the great luxurious room, where it looked cool and dark.
He was hot, and weary with doing nothing. There was a
book lying uncut on a table near him, he peeped into it
and found it was all about a lady's adventures in Japan
—the kind of book he revelled in, although he was so
young. He took up his father's quaint old Spanish
paper-knife and cut the leaves, and was soon lost in the
adventures of the plucky traveller. He was so engrossed that he did not hear the carriage drive up to the
door, or observe his stepmother sail into the room and
ring the bell for tea.

It was his father's voice, speaking in low, soft tones, that
roused him and at last recalled him from an "unbeaten
track" to a consciousness of his surroundings.

He looked up and saw Mr. Fitzgerald reclining on one of
the green plush chairs. He had drawn his wife to him,
and she sat gracefully on the arm of the chair, one of her
white jewelled hands caressing his.

"How lovely you are, my darling," he murmured,
gazing at her fondly. "Your hair is like ripe corn in the
sunshine."

"That's just how he used to talk to her," thought the
desolate boy in his corner. "How can he forget her so
soon? Oh! if he was talking to her now, I should be
sitting at their feet."

The heart-ache this reflection brought on was almost

insufferable. He sprang from his seat with the intention of rushing from the room He did not think of the book on his knees, and it fell to the ground, making his step-mother start.

"I had no idea any one was there," she exclaimed.

"What do you mean by hiding up like that?" his father asked, angrily. "I am astonished that you can find nothing better to do than play the eavesdropper."

"I was reading, and did not see you come in," he faltered.

"And who gave you permission to read that book? You have cut it disgracefully. I shall insist on your asking your mother's leave before you take up books that are very unsuitable for you to read, and spoil them in that way."

"Oh, Edward, I am sure I don't know what sort of books are suitable or not. He is such a precocious child," said the beautiful stepmother with her same little laugh.

Mike knew then that his "giant" was not subdued even yet. He felt a rushing feeling in his head, his eyes filled with burning tears, and his cheeks flamed.

"Why did you have me here at all? You don't love me, or want me," he said passionately. "You never have been a kind father to me since *she* went to heaven. I will go back to Aunt Nancy. *She* loves me. I tried to forgive you, but I never shall now. I will run away now, this very minute! You won't miss me, or care."

"Certainly if you are in the habit of behaving like this, you will be no loss," Mr. Fitzgerald said, coldly.

He ran bare-headed through the grounds, not heeding the threatening sky. It was still and black all round him. He alternately jumped and slid down a grassy slope leading to the sea, and flung himself on a strip of hard sand, on either side of which rose huge unclimbable rocks, so that the tiny cove was only accessible from above. The drowsy murmur of the leaden coloured sea soothed Mike, and his anger died within him.

"Oh, mother! I cannot bear any more. I must give up the battle after all. What have I said to him? Awfully wicked things. I am sorry now, but I can never tell him so. Oh, mother, mother, if God would only let me die!"

His heavy lids, swollen with crying, dropped over his weary eyes, and with the lullaby the little rippling waves sang to him as they crept nearer and nearer, he fell asleep.

In his dreams he saw his mother standing at the end of a long path, thickly strewn with flowers that surpassed all the flowers of earth for beauty. She smiled at him, and his head stopped throbbing and aching, and his heart was light, and he cried for joy. He felt the soft flowers under his feet, and said, "Mother, I am coming, but I don't seem to walk; it's like floating." She smiled again, and once more he felt that buoyant, joyous feeling, as if his soul were being carried up very high. Then when he got as it seemed quite near to her, and thought every moment he would be in her arms, she turned her head away, and said, "Not yet." "I must come to you now, I am so close to you," he cried. "Oh, don't send me away." But she pointed to two dim figures; they were his father and his step-mother standing somewhere very far off. "Not yet," she said again in clear distinct tones. "He loves you, dear; go and be brave a little longer." She passed out of his sight, and the vision of bright flowers faded away.

* * * *

At half-past seven Mr. and Mrs. Fitzgerald sat down to dinner.

"Ring again, Harris," Mr. Fitzgerald said, when he was half-way through his soup, looking uneasily at Mike's empty place.

"If you please, sir, the young gentleman is not at home," Harris replied.

"There is going to be a terrific storm. If he is out in it, Heaven knows what may happen to him!" and much to the surprise of the formal Harris, his master rose from the table and looked anxiously out of the window.

"You need not be alarmed, Edward. He will have reached Halminster by this time," said his wife, calmly.

"Nonsense! He has not gone to Halminster. He had no money. Besides, I saw him take an exactly opposite direction. I fear he is on the shore."

"One of the servants can be sent, I suppose, to bring him home."

The meaningless little laugh which followed up this remark, as it did most of the fair speaker's speeches, was inexpressibly annoying to Mr. Fitzgerald at that moment.

"I shall go myself," he answered decidedly. "Fetch me my coat, Harris."

Harris put down an *entrée* on the sideboard with a disgusted face, and obeyed, while his mistress shrugged her pretty shoulders impatiently.

Mr. Fitzgerald almost instinctively bent his footsteps in the direction of the little cove. He was just in time. The treacherous ocean that had lulled the boy to sleep, wanted now to rock him on its restless breast, and the waves were already beginning to play round his limp, tired little legs. A flash of sheet lightning gave an almost deathly hue to the sleeping features as Mr. Fitzgerald knelt by his side, calling on him to wake.

"Father," he said, opening his eyes. "The giant *is* killed at last. I forgive you; please forgive me and love me!"

"My own dear boy," was all Mr. Fitzgerald could say

He carried him tenderly home, the thunder muttering all round them, and drops the size of florins splashing on their heads.

"We shall never misunderstand each other again, father," Mike said afterwards.

"I trust not, my dear son!" answered the father.

May Aunt Nancy come and see me sometimes?"

"As often as she likes."

"Oh, now I am really happy," he said.

And so Mike finished his first campaign.

THE END.

PRINTED BY PURNELL AND SONS
PAULTON (SOMERSET) AND LONDON